MW00325892

Other Books by John Reeves

A BEACH OF STRANGERS

TRIPTYCH

THE ARITHMETIC OF LOVE

MURDER BY MICROPHONE

CRYPTIC CROSSWORD
(June 14)

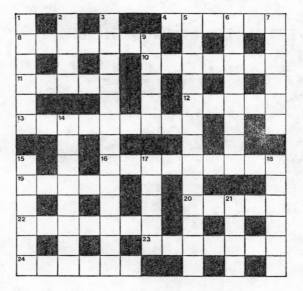

40 MINUTE TEST

ACROSS
4. Tinker, tailor? No, Curtainmaker? Maybe. Writer? Yes. (6)
8. Strike the lady after start of trip to that place. (7)
10. Forever led astray in four directions. (7)
11. Encore sounds like an advantage. (5)
12. Slain, formerly. With a hammer? (5)
13. A dime's worth? Well, almost. (4,5)
16. It isn't only a da capo aria begins here. (3,3,3)
19. If the order goes out, a burglar will come. (5)
20. This orange is not ultra-marine, but sounds quasi-marine. (5)
22. Skating's contribution to the language of danger. (4,3)
23. Thin parliamentarians? (7)
24. Roost for a night-hawk? (3–3)

DOWN
1. Stress the trains with the caboose in front. (6)
2. A liar coins a word. (4)
3. In this at the eleventh hour. (3,4,2,4)
5. His pose is thoughtful, but he never says what he thinks. (6,7)
6. The present lacks two directions, but gains two hundred and one: good place for a cop. (8)
7. A relative goes out of her way not to co-operate. (6)
9. By the sound of it precipitation is the rule here. (5)
14. This play of clerical origin usually focuses on a lay figure. (8)
15. It's said little Edward first sat awry. (6)
17. If you this a mirror, you'd see this endlessly. (5)
18. A language to shine with. (6)
21. To this away is always confused. (4)

MURDER
BY MICROPHONE

John Reeves

1978
Doubleday Canada Limited
Toronto, Canada
Doubleday & Company, Inc.
Garden City, New York

All the characters in this book are fictional, and no reference is intended to any person living or dead. Several of the characters are represented as working for the Canadian Broadcasting Corporation, which is a real institution.[1] I do not suggest, however, that the CBC, as portrayed here, resembles the CBC as it is in real life: it would be foolish to contend that all CBC programs are absurd and that all CBC officers are inept or villainous; I have merely drawn an imaginary portrait of what the CBC might be like if that were the case.

[1] Across the road from the real-life CBC radio building in Toronto is a motel, with a bar and dining-room much frequented by broadcasters. In this book there is also a motel across the road from the radio building. I particularly wish to state that the derogatory opinions here published about the food and drink served at this fictional motel do not in any way refer to the food and drink served at the real-life motel.

Footnote to footnote: This book is full of footnotes. Readers who prefer to skip them will not miss any essential clues.

Library of Congress Cataloging in Publication Data

Reeves, John, 1926–
  Murder by microphone.

  I. Title.
PZ4.R3317Mu 1978   [PR9199.3.R425]   813'.5'4
ISBN: 0-385-14217-X
Library of Congress Catalog Card Number 78–8216

In memory of the late John Drainie
the foremost radio artist of our time

MURDER BY MICROPHONE

ONE

Tuesday, 9:00–9:30A.M.

ON THE MORNING of Tuesday, June 14, at nine o'clock, when Betsy Vulpitude arrived at work, the large leather chair at the desk of the Toronto office of the general manager of CBC radio was occupied, as usual, by a corpse. However, on this particular morning, the corpse did not emit the usual flat and slightly nasal greeting: instead, it rested its head on the blotter and said nothing at all. Also on the blotter was a small pool of blood, and three interested flies were the only signs of life. Miss Vulpitude screamed once, loudly, and sat down on the floor.

If this had happened at half-past nine, her scream would doubtless have brought help, or at least enquiries. Unfortunately, no one else had yet arrived at work, in the executive offices. Elsewhere, in several studios and a few production offices, the AM and FM staffs were hard at work, respectively embalming 27,856 motorists in Welk and mystifying 1.5 housewives with Stockhausen. But the separation between programs and program directors was physical as well as intellectual: they were not merely worlds apart; they occupied different buildings. As a result, her cry fell on deaf ears.[1]

Miss Vulpitude, after a moment's reflection, was glad that this was so. It was not for nothing she had built up a reputation as the Dragon Lady of TRASH (Television-Radio Administration & Sales Headquarters): to be found all a-skitter on the broadloom and yelping like a Sealyham would be neither seemly nor in character. She got up, smoothed her dress, and resumed her customary poise. Then, efficiently and without delay, she double-checked that nobody else was in the room, ascertained that her boss really was dead, and telephoned the police.

After which, while she waited, she lit a cigarette, arranged for the commissionaire to guard the door, and composed her mind. The last of these tasks was the hardest: horror and agitation were quelled easily enough, but what she could not repress was the thought that whoever had killed Henry Midden had bestowed a giant favour on the corporation in particular and the country in general; vaguely Miss Vulpitude felt this response was indecent in the face of sudden death, but somehow the decencies of life seemed to have no more connection now with the late general manager than when he was still alive—"Henry," a small voice within her kept saying, "it serves you right."

She was still extinguishing this blunt but honest thought, and her cigarette, when the police arrived. They came, like sneezing, by instalments. First, the constabulary, in a squad car headlong, with hopeful notebooks and firing questions, diffident with guns. Then in an unmarked car, the divisional doctor, expert on violence though not much else. Finally, the detectives, in orthodox suits and sideburns, at 9:25: thus they exactly resembled the middle rank of executive assistants, who always wore orthodox suits and sideburns and checked in at

[1] There were those willing to assert that her cry would have fallen on deaf ears even if the executives had been *in situ*. But that was purely internecine sarcasm and, as such, lies outside the scope of this report.

14

9:25;[2] and so, for once, they achieved the sleuth's perpetual desire, invisibility.

They were two, frequently paired: an Inspector Coggin and a Sergeant Sump; between them they had had thirty-three years on Homicide.[3] Each alone was capable. As a pair they were unrivalled. This was largely due to their having complementary talents, the one supplying what the other lacked; and to their knowing it. But their successes also stemmed, in part, from the deceptive impression they made on the unwary.

Miss Vulpitude, for instance, sized them up wrong from the start. She was usually an astute judge of character. But, like most people, she was willing to go by first impressions until she had reason to doubt them. Her initial response to the two detectives was based on looks, bearing, and manner. And these seemed to indicate an almost perfect bringing to life of stock figures. Inspector Coggin was sparely built and trimly clad; penetrating eyes hinted at a sharp insight into personality; and a certain suavity of discourse bespoke a wide acquaintance with the ways of the world—here, apparently, was that criminological virtuoso, brilliant as flashbulbs, who at the drop of a deerstalker would conjure up elegant solutions to the tangled problems humanity forever set him. On the other hand, Sergeant Sump was plainly just the plodder: he sat in his suit like

[2] The suits proclaimed whose side these bureaucrats were on. The sideburns suggested, though, that they had an eye to the future too. But it was the hour which was all-important: for there is a hierarchy of arrivals; 9:20 is tacitly ordained for assistants to assistants, 9:25 for executive assistants, and 9:30 for executives—this observed, all can then adjourn for coffee until the mandatory ten o'clock meeting, the Meeting to Plan Meetings.

[3] This exceeded by thirty-two years and 364 days the length of time that the late general manager of CBC radio had ever spent in a broadcasting studio. Taxpayers may draw their own conclusions. Before they do so, however, it must in fairness be added that the late general manager was unquestionably a hard worker: he came to the office on time and stayed till 5:00 and in between wrote many forceful, though ungrammatical, memos (Miss Vulpitude rewrote them without comment—and collected the more splendid bloopers in a secret file); he was thought by some to be more interested in power than in programs, but those who thought so were plainly biased, being themselves more interested in programs than in power.

a farmer at a funeral; large, blunt hands suggested no subtle intellect; he was amiable and solid and quiet, and inspired the
sort of trust which made it easy for people to talk to him—
even suspects. As a working team, they reinforced these ap-
praisals: Sergeant Sump did nearly all the interviewing (much
of it seemingly routine) while Inspector Coggin hovered in the
background, like a dangerous eminence, interjecting only the
occasional sharp question, to which his colleague deferred. And
their respective ranks, finally, confirmed the whole picture, in
the mind of most: there is, in almost everyone, a snobbery
which assumes, automatically, that evident brain by rights
should outrank evident brawn; Coggin was evidently Sump's
superior, in every way.[4]

This estimate was not made only by Miss Vulpitude: it was
shared, at first, by almost everyone who had dealings with the
investigators; it was, however, thoroughly mistaken.

Andrew Coggin, for instance, was a gifted man, but not in
the way he appeared. His main talent was for reducing events
to a series of abstractions: solving crimes, so far as he was concerned, was simply a matter of processing the data until they
assumed the rational order of algebra, and then plodding away
at them until they yielded an answer; cold analysis was his
forte. His weak point was people: he lacked relish for men and
women and children in all their muddle and inconsistency; life,
on the whole, made him uncomfortable. This perhaps
stemmed from a boyhood which had been first lonely and then
shy. Like many shy men, he sought cerebral pleasures to make
up for what he missed in human warmth, and learnt also to
cultivate social aplomb as a form of self-protection. His well-cut
clothes, his adroit turn of phrase, these were an armour against
the anarchy of persons. Even the piercing look in his chilly
blue eyes, which so many ascribed to a daunting power of ap-

[4] See chapter 28 of *Der Sherlockholmesismuskult der Polizeiwirklichkeit
gegenüber* by Ewald Krummhorn, a statistical critique of lay attitudes to
criminology: to equate genius with advancement (or vice versa) is
evidently as absurd in police stations as it would be in radio stations;
though one is bound to add that this analogy is less fair to German
broadcasting than it is to the CBC.

praisal, was nothing more than impatience, a wish to be alone and to cogitate. When he was alone, the cogitation was of a high order. But the personal defect, the crippling reserve, remained. No one had ever called him Sandy.

By contrast, Fred Sump had never in his life been addressed as Frederick. From a tousled urchin and an outdoors youth he had grown into a shirt-sleeves man, extroverted, able to get on well with anyone. His conversation was casual, friendly, unmemorable. He seemed more interested in drawing others out than in pushing himself forward. These traits, in most people's eyes, added up to a stereotype: the comfortable unimaginative man, who could be relied on for common sense and for routine, but whose perceptions would be limited and pedestrian; a cop. In fact, this persona was little more than a mask (though none the less sincere for that): behind it, was an almost limitless curiosity about people and a vast capacity to learn what made them tick; unsuspected by all but his colleagues. People, indeed, were Sergeant Sump's forte. Unlike Inspector Coggin, he lacked the flair for plodding through abstract analysis, for cold logic. But he did have remarkable humane powers: perspicacity, experience, and intuition; and, of these, his intuition was his most trenchant weapon, for it was based on a real sensitivity to character and led him often to unearth quirks of motive or attitude which no merely deductive process could suppose existed.

Thus it was that these two men complemented one another's gifts in ways quite different from what appeared on the surface. And the longer they worked together, the more each appreciated what the other had to offer. Inspector Coggin valued greatly his sergeant's talent for empathy (only he would have spotted the connection between the kitchen knife and the Player's cigarette package which had identified the psychopath in the Case of the Amputated Vagina): indeed, like many shy intellectuals, he envied him it. Sergeant Sump admired no less his inspector's talent for computation (only he could have sifted through the endless contradictions in the case of the Five Compulsive Liars until they yielded their fatal nugget of invol-

17

untary truth): and his respect, too, was tinged with envy; the misplaced envy of the unlettered for those with university degrees. This mutual esteem made them formidable partners. And they were both shrewd enough to exploit the tendency of strangers to jump to wrong conclusions.[5] Inspector Coggin was not averse to being Poirot-Maigret in the suspects' minds if it would encourage them in the right direction: ideally, they would become so concerned about relationships and personalities that they would lapse into carelessness about times and places and weather and food and money; and it was in this mundane field of particular evidence that many solutions lay. Correspondingly, Sergeant Sump was perfectly content to be taken for a conscientious dullard if it would catch the suspects off guard: ideally, they would become so attentive to trivial questions of fact that they would let slip revealing statements about themselves or one another; and in any investigation where clue and character are concerned, it is a moot point which is the chicken and which is the egg.

Usually, then, they got off to a good start, simply because of the erroneous impression they made—and fostered. And, in this, even the accidents of seniority and physique abetted them: for Coggin, who looked like a sharp comer in his mid-thirties, was actually fifty-two and had achieved his inspectorate late by sheer perseverance; whereas Sump, who played the sergeant role like a universal father-figure, was not yet forty but already in line for promotion.

There was a lot more to Miss Vulpitude, too, than at first met the eye. But it is not surprising that when the two detectives arrived it was Sergeant Sump who inspired in her an immediate sense of trust and Inspector Coggin who left her feeling wary. And this wariness sharpened into anxiety as she suddenly realised that, for the time being at least, she would probably fill the role of prime suspect.

[5] As to their standing among professional colleagues, nobody meant it unkindly when they were nicknamed Laurel and Hardy. By contrast, there did seem to be an element of malice in the nicknames attached to the CBC vice-presidents: King Kong, Caliban, Madame Defarge, Dopey, Cock Robin, Dr. Goebbels, God, Sweet William, and Mack the Knife.

TWO

Tuesday, 9:30–12:00

PROGRAM SCHEDULE #1: *Tuesday* 9:30–12:00

9:30 "Kaffee Klatsch," with host Delmore Vance: conversation and musical éclairs. This morning's guests: August Plinth, president of the Yukon Chapter of the I-Like-Ludwig Club; Dementia Wilcox, spokesman for SLIB (the Society for the Liberation of Budgerigars): and Joe Wurst, sausage-taster.

10:00 News[1]

10:04 "Bodtime," with Mildred Bodsworth, a morning magazine for drop-ins. Today: for consumers, "News about Yogurt" from Groin Harbour, Newfoundland; for concerned citizens, "Alderperson at Large," with Constance Lautmund; for homemakers, "Horsemeat: an alternative," by Xaviera Welsh; and throughout the program, for music-lovers, the Ballbearings, as recorded last month at the folk festival in Temple, B.C.

11:30 Ontario Schools Broadcast: Grade Twelve English: "How to spell CAT," an advanced look at new concepts in audio-visual semantics: with William L. All-

[1] News on the hour every hour had been inaugurated on AM some ten years beforehand, in a misguided attempt to keep news-hungry listeners from switching to other stations. The error in this policy was the assumption that CBC listeners could not contain their appetites until the next full news report, but instead had to be given snacks to hold them over. These quick batches of headlines, which did not merit being described as bulletins, were known in the profession as "news-burps."

Murder by Microphone

ways, B.Ed., Assistent Proffesor of Aplied Linguisticks, Excellsior Corespondence Colege, Mucus, Ontario.

9:30   "Current and Choice," a weekly critique of some newly published books. Here is this week's list: FICTION: *Pieces of Tale* by Chester Bounce, a collection of short stories (Rhine & Rowse, $5.00) reviewed by Agatha Duct. VERSE: *Foundry Poems* by Joe Gorbal (Krapp & Co., $1.25) reviewed by Septimus Lavender. RELIGION: *Interdenominational Dialogue* by Wilbur Smeech, B.D. (Limbo Press, $7.50) reviewed by Canon Hinge-Hackett, D.D. ROMANCE: *Paradise Unbound* by Emily Fawcett Fillmore (Heimweh, Sousa, Lafontaine, $4.75) reviewed by Porfirio Mountjoy. AUTOBIOGRAPHY: *Strumpet Voluntary* by Gloria Beddoes (ffrench & Swallow, $5.00) reviewed by Sigmund Crotch. Producer: Eunice Pringle.

10:00   *Glossolalia,* a radiophonic oratorio in three styles and two acts by Theodore Plunge, conducted by Wlodzimierz Szczvrko: featuring the Serenata String Orchestra, the Ten Orgasms (rock group), and special effects from the tape-lab of Omega University; with soloists Beata Achtung, soprano, Marvis Feckle, stovepipes, and Wayne Sprockett, synthesiser. During the intermission, a talk by Egerton Snape: "New Directions in Mixed-Media Quadrisonics." Producer: Conway Spleiss (recorded at a public performance last March in the Ducharme Memorial Hall, St. Prépuce, P.Q.).

SERGEANT SUMP WAS, however, disinclined to suspect Miss Vulpitude. She was too convincingly straightforward. Their first interview was admittedly brief: she described finding the body and answered the immediately necessary questions about next of kin, and that was that for the time being; but even in five minutes her manner had tended to clear her—she simply wasn't the type.

Or, rather, wasn't one of the many types. And Sergeant Sump had seen most of them, if not all. They varied greatly, but still certain generalizations were possible. For instance, murder could be divided into two large categories: premeditated, and spontaneous. People who killed on the spur of the moment either remained flustered or else assumed an abnormal calm: neither response carried the ring of truth. People who had planned a killing were usually more plausible: seemingly co-operative, their story pat; but they, too, lacked the authentic demeanour of innocence (the halting, incomplete replies, the inconsistencies, the embarrassment, the anxiety), because it lay beyond the scope of their imagining or their powers of enactment. Other people, in most cases, were not guilty.

These generalizations, of course, were far from valid in other fields. The fraud squad, for one, would have little use for intuitive detection: con men are caught by hard evidence, and without it there's little to go on; their whole trade rests on the ability to observe human nature minutely and to adopt a trustworthy mien. But con men, by definition, are non-violent. And their nimble sensitivity to character is a trait almost universally lacking in violent criminals. In the latter, somehow, it's as though the violence were an expression of that lack: they fail to relate to people; therefore people must pay.

At least, that was true of career criminals with a violent record. And plenty of them ended up on a homicide charge. Most murderers, though, were not career criminals. Their lives were peaceful, law-abiding, unremarkable. Then suddenly, one day, they killed: irrationally, without skill; and all their friends are astounded. Sergeant Sump had heard it time and again: "But, Officer, it's impossible . . . he was always so polite . . . such a quiet person . . . no, they never had fights that we knew of . . ." And the faces matched the reputations: bland, drab, anonymous; more pathetic than vicious. He winced every time he looked at the photographs: for here if anywhere, he knew, was the real evidence of our flawed nature; here, but for the grace of luck, went Everyman, not villain but victim, a prey to some inner pain he could not bear. The nagged husband, driven beyond endurance; the battered wife, desperate for escape; the meek, frustrated clerk, a man of cocoa and resignation, breaking out in whisky and unforeseeable rage; all sorts and conditions of men and women, willing to take their universal share of disappointment and routine, but each of them wrecked in the end on some impassable reef of humiliation, or debt, or sexual jealousy: no one could ever be sure it wouldn't happen to him. And because the act of killing, in such cases, was so radically out of character, the killers, when faced with what they had done, usually confessed. Or, if they lied, lied badly.

Sergeant Sump tried to keep an open mind. He knew the improbable could never be discounted. Most homicides were squalidly similar; most investigations were humdrum; most killers were average citizens. But every now and then a mutation would occur; the trail would stretch the mind; and the culprit would be exceptional—oddly motivated, or unusually astute and inventive. These murders were nearly always premeditated, and the murderers were very often of superior intelligence; sometimes, in addition, they were psychopaths, which gave them a double advantage: on the one hand it enabled them to lie with no sense of falsehood and to assume without unease whatever personality was convenient, and on the other hand it so far removed them from human norms that their behaviour was incomprehensible, their minds impenetrable. Such cases were only cracked by solid facts, never by insight into character: and even when they were solved, the mystery remained, the mystery of the murderer who can be caught but not understood; all other mental and emotional disorders are perversions of normal states, and those who suffer them merely caricatures of ourselves, but the psychopath is utterly alien, a species wholly apart.

That was the possibility which forever haunted him: that an apparently open-and-shut case would turn out to be a trap; that the obvious motives, the plentiful clues, and the handy suspect were all planted, were all a misleading cover for something else, for some unsuspected genius with a sound alibi and no imaginable motive. It could always happen. He could never afford to dismiss it.

But having an open mind, Sergeant Sump reflected, is not the same as having a vacant one.[2] He was bound to remember that just possibly Miss Vulpitude might combine the morals of a cobra with the cunning of a vixen and a chameleon's power of camouflage. But that did not prevent his knowing, from experience, that here was a lady who could almost certainly be taken at face value.

The lime-green linen ensemble, in itself, said nothing—ex-

---

[2] The distinction was one which occurred to him frequently: but it had never before occurred to anyone in that particular room: intellects, in the office of the General Manager of the CBC, were both closed and empty.

cept that she felt no need to mimic the young in frayed jeans and a T-shirt with HANG IN THERE printed across the nipples. Likewise the neat grey hair-do simply stated that she knew who she was and where she belonged. But other things told more: a wrinkling smile entirely free of malice, eyes that were unevasive and in tune with what she was saying, and a voice apparently not tailored for effect; alone, none of these evidences would have meant very much, but taken together they reassured him.

She had identified the body: without making a scene. She had related her discovery of it: and was clearly still shaken by the experience. She had provided the name and address and telephone number of the victim's widow: and had managed to intimate, without being either catty or callous, that Mrs. Midden would not be prostrated with unendurable grief. She resembled—for a moment he could not place the memory, and then it came back to him—she resembled all those platoon sergeants in the army who kept the operation going while the green subalterns bumbled:[3] chances were, she would know more about everyone connected with the case than all the rest of them put together. An invaluable witness.

That had been half an hour ago. Since then, a man had been assigned to break the news to Mrs. Midden; to begin investigating his private life; to report on the likelihood of his having incurred any serious enmities away from his work. The president of the CBC had been phoned and said he would fly in from Ottawa at once. Requests had gone out to various executives and program heads for interviews about their late and, it seemed, not much lamented General Manager (Miss Vulpitude

[3] The resemblance, he discovered later, was only true in part. Like a sergeant, she made up for deficiencies above. But in the CBC, a Miss Vulpitude would never be assigned to a mere subaltern: green executives had to make do with novice stenos possessed of little typing and less shorthand; rather, she would work for a senior officer, whose lifelong incompetence had gotten him kicked further and further upstairs. Thus it was, in those days, that her cement (and that of her kind) saved the entire structure from ignominious collapse. And this, however unplanned, was the sole piece of managerial prudence on record.

had been invaluable here: her lists of who attended what regular or occasional meetings saved them hours of digging around: but she went much further than simply supplying names; she provided quick impressions of everyone's temperament and talents, impressions that seemed to be neither rancorous nor partisan, and managed to suggest, without openly saying so, that some people on her lists were only marginally involved with H.M. as the deceased had been derisively acronymed, and therefore might have much less to offer than others in the way of information or help). The medical report would not take long. And the usual futile search had begun for a readable set of fingerprints.[4]

Meanwhile, much of the morning could profitably be spent on preliminary spadework. The whole main floor had been sealed off and placed under guard as soon as the police had arrived. But that was now modified: only the general manager's suite was kept under closure; and even so, in the outer office, Miss Vulpitude was asked to remain at her desk, to receive and annotate phone calls and to help deal with scheduled or unscheduled visitors. The rest of the floor was returned to normal use. This was done partly to allow people to go about their ordinary business, but mainly in order to keep the investigation in a low key. In Sergeant Sump's view, which the inspector endorsed, a police presence should be as unassuming as possible: that way, innocent witnesses were more generally unperturbed and helpful; and the guilty were sometimes lulled.

The first witnesses were routine, necessary, and sleepy: night watchmen and cleaning staff, untimely ripped from sleep. Their contribution was useful but purely negative. No one had

---

[4] Readers of detective fiction have been led to believe that every physical crime, if it is not committed in gloves, leaves a clear spoor for the man with the powder and the magnifying glass. In real life, few surfaces yield results, and regular methods seldom obtain a legible print: moreover, little extra is achieved by resorting to the laborious and expensive advanced methods which are available if the case is thought important enough to warrant using them. A recent survey of property crimes in one jurisdiction showed that prints were obtained in only 3 per cent of the cases.

been seen entering or leaving Henry Midden's office, or its vicinity, in the course of the night: anyone who wanted to do so could easily accomplish it without being observed; no sounds, violent or otherwise, had been heard from his office, and anyway nothing unusual could have been noticed after 7:30, as the cleaning staff had left the building by that time to go over to the next building and clean up in the studios and production offices. Yes, this was the invariable pattern of their work: the administrative offices could usually be counted on to be empty and available for cleaning after five-thirty, except when a retirement party or a press party went on till seven; whereas the studios were often in use till eleven-thirty, and some producers were known to work through the night, from time to time, in the editing rooms upstairs, clogging the floors with a mixed detritus of cigarette butts, paper cups, and excised tape.[5] No, there was nothing unusual about the general manager's car having been already on the executive parking lot when the attendant arrived at work in the early morning: no one else of his rank ever came in that early, but he did several times a year; how often, oh about twice a month at a guess.

Both officers filed this fact away for future reference. To Inspector Coggin it was a simple objective fact, without any known further meaning, to be stored along with others, but not interpreted, until enough facts had been gathered for their patterns to start emerging. Sergeant Sump, however, saw it principally as a fact which might shed light on the victim's character; and in the victim's character, often, there lay a clue to the vic-

[5] The cynic who said that the best thing about television was the commercials might well have added that radio left many a good moment on the editing-room floor. The bad takes from music sessions were no great loss, nor were the wooden attempts of academics and clergy to read the written word or the inarticulate attempts of interviewees to say what was on their minds: but the fluffs of actors, with the consequent oaths and hilarity, could only with sorrow be cut out; many a drama producer was known to regret that he lacked the time to save them and compile them into a program, even though such a program could only be for private use —that much swearing wasn't allowed on the air unless it was part of an avant-garde poem.

tim's death. As yet he had little to go on: before the day was out a firm picture would form in his mind of a man not much liked or respected, who had risen by understanding the processes of power rather than by any devotion to broadcasting or gift for it; but at this preliminary stage he had no means of knowing whether this occasional habit of industriousness at the crack of dawn was in character or not. Eventually it turned out that it was in character: by establishing a reputation for nocturnal overwork, Henry Midden had an acceptable excuse to offer his mistress (he had long since given up lying to his wife) when he wanted to be absent from her bed in pursuit of whatever newly attractive female was willing to advance her career by spreading her legs for a lecher;[6] sometimes he would emerge from these amours at 3 A.M. or so, and then, rather than head home, he'd go straight in to the office and dictate a tapeful of memos and letters for Miss Vulpitude, thus freeing the rest of his day for those meetings and confrontations and deals which were so much more important and interesting to him than correspondence could ever be, let alone programs.

This practice of occasionally coming in early had a clearly probable bearing on the case, since it might well have been known to the murderer and have provided him with his opportunity. But the private ramifications turned out to have no bearing on the case at all: the officer who was assigned to dig into Henry Midden's private life never did unearth anything of value. He had early realized the huge extent of the task ahead (such a womanizer, in the middle ages, would have to have

---

[6] H.M. had a fixation on large breasts, but was defensive about it, and one of his women triggered a lasting hostility in him because of it: like many of the well endowed, she had a sense of humor on the subject, a sense of the infantility in the lust she inspired, and one night she made an unforgiveable crack about the transactional aspect of their affair by referring to it as "a sale of two titties"; this allusion to the one novel by Dickens which H.M. had ever heard of did not amuse him, and she failed to receive the promotion she felt she'd earned. A better man would have gallantly replied "Ah yes, but 'tis a far far better thing I do than I have ever done" and instantly remounted. But H.M. was neither good nor gallant.

had as a motto "Semper tumens," "Forever erect") and had phoned in to say so. But none of the women he traced apparently bore Mr. Midden any deep or lasting malice: he seemed, rather, to have aroused a unanimous and dismissive contempt, and to have been put out of mind, like a bad taste. Nor was there any evidence of anything approaching homicidal jealousy in any of the men who were indirectly involved, the other lovers or husbands: so far as he could tell, most of them weren't in the know; and those who were seemed not to care greatly. The officer concerned never did reach the end of the trail: the case was solved before he could do so; but as he remarked to his wife, if it had gone on much longer, he'd have been in for a bad case of vicarious sexual fatigue.

Meanwhile, the medical report had been phoned in. Death was estimated to have occurred between 11 P.M. and 2 A.M., and was due to a severe blow on the right temple, preceded by a less severe blow on the left temple. The latter had caused no scarification of the outer skin at all, and with the former the exterior laceration was not extensive. This suggested a weapon without any sharp edges or corners, at least at the point of impact. No object of this sort had been left at the scene of the crime, and none was found in the vicinity by the constables combing the area. This was just as the inspector and the sergeant had expected: no drops of blood were on the carpet between the desk and the door, and that suggested the killer had been able to wrap the weapon up in something before leaving (possibly in whatever it had been concealed in when he arrived); if so, he might have been able to safely take it a considerable distance before disposing of it.

Not only was there no blood on the carpet, there was no apparent sign of a struggle. This indicated, though not conclusively, that the victim had known the killer and either had met him/her there by appointment or come there with him/her or else had not been surprised or alarmed when he/she turned up, presumably with a plausible reason for being there. The possibility could not be ruled out that the killer was a stranger off the street, killing at random for no apparent reason and leaving afterwards no apparent trace; but this was at least unlikely. It was much more reasonable to suppose a connection between the killer and the victim, a connection having something to do with the victim's private or professional life. Given the location, Inspector Coggin tended to favor the latter idea, though without any bias towards either of its variants: premeditated murder or impromptu. But if he was right, someone in Midden's professional life had been capable of killing, for one reason or another. The possibilities were endless, in terms of human behaviour, and were perhaps best left to Sergeant Sump: sudden ungovernable rage, long-nursed hatred, ambition, a rational or an unreasoning fear, jealousy, perhaps even a power struggle gone wrong; these were only the crude and obvious labels for some of those darker recesses of the psyche which the Inspector found so hard to cope with. But where there was a motive there were also means and opportunity. He sighed. He was good at this kind of work. But he did not expect it to be quick or easy.

He cast his eye reflectively around the room. Was it possible that it contained a suitable weapon and they had overlooked it? Over the mantelpiece a Victorian duenna stared severely down, framed in gilt, who once had ruled here as sole arbiter of taste and conduct, eighty years ago, when young daughters of money were sent to these premises, then a boarding school, to acquire the shallow intellectual but complex social stamp of ladies: behind her canvas gaze no blunt instrument lurked; they had looked. On the hearth below her there were no fire irons, for the grate had long since been bricked up, effectively blocking the chimney as a hiding place. On either side of the hearth, two built-in cupboards contained nothing but tapes and papers. The lighting fixtures, trendily modern and grotesquely at odds with the architecture, were unadaptable to homicide, at least of an unelectric sort. Floor-length drapes, hideously imprinted with the CBC's puce and orange symbol, certainly might stifle the spirit or horrify the mind, but were hardly likely to produce

31

a fatal contusion of the brain. The chairs were of a design
uniformly supplied to all senior executives irrespective of other
decor: cunningly padded, they gave off uncivil exhalations
when sat upon, and the fake black leather caused most occu-
pants to sweat uncomfortably at the back of the thighs after
five minutes; they were monstrosities, but none of them could
conceivably be picked up and wielded as a hammer. The same
was true of the wastepaper basket, an Art Nouveau imitation
constructed apparently of wicker but actually of plastic and
painted an unappetizing white, like blancmange. Handy
lengths of plumber's pipe were not lying around in the corners,
of lethal cast; the ashtrays were all lightweight, and nothing on
or within the desk had any offensive potential. As an arsenal,
the room was a void. There was not even a newspaper.[7]

It was now almost lunchtime. For CBC employees this was a
term understood to have many meanings. Clock-punchers had
to take it literally: sixty minutes. Office staffs varied: some had
old-fashioned supervisors, who gave everyone a choice of noon
to one or one to two but allowed no extra; others, more loosely
run, could count on eighty or ninety minutes. Executives, who
were not supervised, varied also: the ambitious took twenty re-
luctant minutes and hurried back to sharpen their knives; the
time-servers took an hour and a half, telling dirty jokes over five
drinks and a cottage-cheese salad before wandering back to
their empty, make-work desks; and the real bosses took two
hours and talked shop. Producers, though, varied most of all:
some didn't arrive till noon, after a late breakfast, and then
worked through till late evening, organizing for themselves at
some point a woolburger-to-go and sludge-with-cream-and-sugar
or a cardboard sandwich and imitation-fruit juice; others took
long, bibulous, and program-related lunches with writers or per-

---

[7] A wartime course in Unarmed Combat had taught Inspector Coggin
that there are nine ways to make a deadly weapon out of a newspaper.
Deadly, that is, to human life—it is not necessary to enrol in such courses
to learn that there are more than nine ways in which most newspapers are
deadly to language.

formers; at least one regularly worked through the lunch hour and went home early, to work off the creative frustrations of his job by writing books.

Inspector Coggin and Sergeant Sump had no set pattern. On slow days at the office they'd go out to eat, separately, at a relaxed pace, as opportunity offered. Out on cases, they were at the mercy of the tempo of the job: if it allowed them to eat, they ate; if not, they went without. The first day on a case of any substance seldom allowed a meal break. But today it looked possible: the preliminary series of investigative interviews was to begin at two o'clock with the president; until then food might perhaps be combined with consideration of the case. Inspector Coggin suggested to Sergeant Sump that he might invite Miss Vulpitude to lunch with him, since she seemed like a useful source and Fred was good at that kind of thing. He himself would try to find someone who could fill him in on the structural organization of CBC management, so that he would know in advance what kind of business relationships were involved when the afternoon's interviews began.[8]

However, before trying to find an interpreter of these mysteries, Inspector Coggin decided, quite on the spur of the moment, to check the dead man's dictaphone. If he had happened to be using it when the murderer arrived, it was just possible it might contain worthwhile evidence. He asked Miss Vulpitude to show him how it worked, and then sat back, with the plug in his ear, to listen. Miss Vulpitude, as she left the room, saw

[8] Inspector Coggin would not ordinarily have been described as a naïve man. But it certainly smacked of naïveté for him to imagine that one lunch hour was enough to grasp the intricacies of CBC bureaucracy: on paper it was neatly organized and clear; in reality it was labyrinthine, and many a middle-rank executive had lost his way in it. Its workings were complicated by the fact that nearly everyone involved knew the system was more than just unwieldy, it was unworkable; so they all sought ways around it. This was easy to do, since nearly all functions were ill defined and, to some extent, overlapped. Certainly titles were no guide to duties, even to the titleholders themselves, let alone to an outsider. What could a mere police officer, then, suppose were the responsibilities of, for instance, the Symbol Co-ordinator (ESD)?

33

him suddenly stiffen into a stilled and grave attention. She went out, wishing with a perfectly natural curiosity that it had occurred to her to check the machine, and closed the door. Two minutes later he was out again in her office, asking how to wind the tape back as he had to get it typed and he didn't want to risk wiping it by hitting the wrong knob. She volunteered to type it up for him herself, but he said no, this was evidence, it would have to be done by a police typist. Miss Vulpitude wound the tape back for him. She felt excluded.

Her disappointment was almost immediately mollified, however. Sergeant Sump, with great affability, invited her to lunch, implying in the course of doing so that he was counting on her for help. This was by no means an empty exchange, on either side: Sergeant Sump wished every case would contain someone like her, objective, co-operative, and with a good memory; she, for her part, was perfectly well aware that what she had to offer in the way of background information was likely valuable and, to some extent, unobtainable elsewhere. They agreed on the dining room in the motel across the road.

They were just about to leave when there was an interruption at the outer door. Someone had arrived for an appointment with Henry Midden, not having heard of the murder, and the constable on duty was telling him that he couldn't go in, and explaining why. They heard his shocked "Good God!" and then Inspector Coggin called out to the constable to send him in anyway, at least into the outer office where they all at the moment happened to be.

"I'm Inspector Coggin," he said, "and this is Sergeant Sump who works with me. I guess you know Miss Vulpitude. You had an appointment to see Mr. Midden?"

"Yes. At noon. About a program conference."

"And you are?"

"Oh, sorry." The man was obviously still flustered. "I'm Michael Sherriff. Radio Drama."

"Mr. Sherriff is one of our senior producers," Miss Vulpitude volunteered, with just a touch of approving emphasis on the word *senior*. Despite her long years in Administration, Miss Vulpitude had a prior loyalty to Programs, where she had begun: and she never lost the belief, to which administrators paid only lip service, that programming was what the CBC ought to be about; and anyone who could survive twenty years in production, as this man had, clearly possessed not only stamina but also a level of competence which made it unnecessary to kick him upstairs.

The two policemen looked at him. A tallish man, with ginger hair turning grey. Blue eyes, with a direct and confident look. Clean-shaven. The pale complexion and poor posture which spoke of an indoors man spending too many hours in closed rooms breathing stale air. Nevertheless a sense of unspent energy. Tobacco stains on the fingers. Open-necked shirt, jacket, pants, and shoes all of an unobtrusive sort that showed no desire to join in the latest or less-than-latest fads of radical chic or psychedelic kitsch. His shoes were not polished.

Inspector Coggin made up his mind. "Look," he said, "if you had the time set aside to spend with Mr. Midden, perhaps in the circumstances you wouldn't mind spending it with me instead. I rather need someone to show me the ropes and give me the low-down on how this place works. Could we have lunch together?"

And so it was arranged. Sherriff would take him on a quick tour of the Administration Building and the Program Building, explaining as much as he could on the way; and then they would go to lunch in the staff cafeteria. The dictaphone typing was assigned to a police steno. And they set out.

THREE

Tuesday, 12:00–1:00

PROGRAM SCHEDULE #2: *Tuesday 12:00–1:00*

12:00 News

12:04 "Midday Matters," a lunchtime magazine of items for
the growing audience, the professional on the farm or
the amateur in his own back yard. Today.
"Mulch" by Ted Soddy.
"How to bed a begonia" by H. P. Cummings.
"Udder Itch: relief is on the way" by Harvey Gris-
wold, D. Pharm.
Musical interludes by Earl Moist and the Lunen-
burgers, plus our regular visit with "Hoot" de Groot.
Livestock prices, feed-grain quotations, bargains in
fertilizer, all the tidbits that make life on the land a
laugh a minute.
Hosted by Myra Snodgrass. Production: Winston Boy-
chuck.

12:40 "Equal Time": host Ramsey Warble introduces guest
speakers on two sides of an argument. This week: "The
political responsibilities of pre-school" by Willard Este:
Mr. Este was NDP candidate during the recent by-elec-
tion in St. Bile, Quebec./"Protecting your child from
the radical left" by Renata Ampleforth: Mrs. Ampleforth is President of 6-S, the Southern Saskatchewan
Society of Sunday School Superintendents.

FM SERVICE

12:00 "The Noon Hour," sixty minutes of classical favourites from the record collector's shelf, chosen by Royce Neely. Tuesday is Opera Day, and the program will include: "Una furtiva lagonda" from *Alfa Romeo e Giulietta* by Alessandro Bugatti, sung by Enrico Maserati; Overture to *El Hispano*, with the Detroit Symphony Orchestra under Frederick Rafael de Suiza; "Bist du mein Benz" from *Porschefal* by Engelbert Lumpenwagen, sung by Mercedes Grosstraubel; Entr'acte from *Les Citroëns* by Hector Renault, with the Orchestre de la Conservatoire Parisienne conducted by Charles Caouette; and Act Two of *De Volvo Non Disputandum*, a twelve-tone music-drama by Igor Ziv, with libretto by W. H. Audi, recorded under a grant from the Edsel Foundation by the original cast of the Alice B. Packard Memorial Theatre production in Austin, Texas, directed by Hubert von Karavan, and starring Astre Desmond, Martha Datsun, Morris Forrester, and Karel Bravura-Škoda.

"THIS," SAID Michael Sherriff, opening a door, "is what is laughingly referred to as a studio. I've brought you here first because this is the key to understanding our whole operation. It's what I guess you'd call 'hard evidence' in your profession."

"Meaning?"

"Meaning that it bears out a lot of what I'll have to tell you. It's the outward and visible sign of an inward and corporate disgrace. In effect, it's why we're in bad shape. I won't bore you with technical detail, but believe me this room bears the same relation to modern broadcasting as a pony trap does to space travel. We're expected to turn out acceptable work, but we're given stone-age tools to do it with."

Inspector Coggin made sympathetic noises, and they emerged.

"Down this corridor, and in one or two other places," his guide continued, "we have eleven program studios. When I arrived, in the fifties, we had twelve. During that time the amount of programming we've produced has remained roughly constant: the production staff has increased slightly, because the work has increased in complexity; but it's fair to say we were, and still are, understaffed. During the same period the administration staff has increased by about five hundred per cent. As a taxpayer, you'd probably agree that bears looking into. Though, of course, that's not what you're here to look into as a policeman."

"Yes and no," Coggin replied. "You never know what might have bearing on a case like this." They had started to climb some stairs, flattening themselves against the wall as an agitated figured dashed by, apparently consisting of head and legs and, in between, a vast precarious pile of tapes. "For instance, I detect in what you say at least irony, if not active resentment. Spread enough of that around, and who knows what it might lead to?"

"You see this as an intramural crime, then, so to speak?"

"It's one of the possibilities." Inspector Coggin noted drily that it was not he who had led the conversation in this direction. "What do you think?"

"Well, obviously it's *one* of the possibilities. I've no idea what kind of animosities Henry Midden may have aroused in his private life—indeed, it's rather hard to imagine his having a private life: that would presuppose a human streak in him, and such an idea's preposterous. Look, I'm sorry to be saying things which must seem to you in rotten bad taste, seeing the man isn't even in his grave yet. But I presume you're more interested in candour than convention. Here's my office. Come on in."

The room was in strong contrast to Henry Midden's office, which was the converted parlour of a Victorian mansion, guaranteed to put visitors on their best behaviour and remind them that the occupant was a person of substance. This office was an eight-by-five cubicle in an attic which had once been the servant's quarters of the girls' boarding school. It was crammed almost to bursting with a desk, two chairs, a filing cabinet, and multitudinous tapes and scripts, on shelves, on the desk, in cardboard boxes, and even on the floor. There was just room to sit down without tripping or knocking anything over.

"On the face of it," Sherriff continued, "your theory stands up. There's a lot of ill-feeling between Production and Administration: every new bureaucrat put on the payroll means that much less budget for programs, that much less to show the taxpayer for his dollar. Mind you, we don't have to get paranoid about it: it takes more bodies to run a business these days than it used to, and some managerial growth has to be expected. But not on this scale. And certainly not of this quality. That's the crux of the matter: the quality. Most people in programs would harbour much less of a grudge if only the administrators we had were good ones: after all, we have to concede the right of management to manage; but this lot isn't even good at the basics of business, let alone providing enlightened leadership. I've survived seven administrations in my time here, and each one's been worse than the last. We've arrived at a point now where it's almost impossible to find anyone in management with a scrap of talent to his name—or brains, or taste, or education."

The phone rang. "Take messages, will you, Mary-Lou?" he bellowed. "I'm busy."

"Okay," a distant soprano responded.

"Sorry to shout," Sherriff apologised. "The intercom doesn't work—never has. Where was I? Oh yes. Well, you can gather from this I feel fairly strongly on the subject. So do a lot of others; though I imagine you won't want to take my word for that. And I guess, for a lot of us, Henry Midden came to symbolise much of what we detest about the way things are run around here. However, before you put me at the top of your list of suspects, closely followed by fifty-five other producers, I guess I ought to tell you why that suspicion would turn out to be groundless. Henry Midden was sixty-four."

Inspector Coggin realized with a start that the flow of talk had stopped. Some response was obviously expected from him. He had no previous experience of drama directors, of the way they expound an interpretative position, arrive (sometimes rather ramblingly) at a point, and then expect from their cast

43

an acquiescent concurrence with it. But the technique did have its parallels in other walks of life, notably in the armed forces, and he recognized it. For a moment, his mind occupied itself with the numeral "sixty-four": this man was old enough to have been active in the era of the sixty-four-dollar question; perhaps some obscure allusion was being made which eluded him. However, he quickly abandoned speculation. The flow would continue if he could just find the right word, the suitably inconclusive word with the right note of interest and willingness to learn. Inspector Coggin had not been an interrogator for thirty years for nothing. He knew the word. "Really?" he said.

"Yes," Sherriff went on, obviously unconscious of what had passed through the inspector's mind. "That means he was due to retire next year. So I doubt if you'll find a producer who was willing to risk murdering him when we'd soon be getting rid of him anyway in the course of nature. A few more months wouldn't make that much difference."

No, Coggin reflected: not to a reasonable man, they wouldn't. But then murder, by definition, is an unreasonable act. Nevertheless, Sherriff's point was well taken. The murder might be an in-house job or it might not.[1] But if it was, then it would be unreasonable to attach too much significance to the resentment or contempt felt for Henry Midden by producers, or anyway by one producer: even if those feelings had reached, in some cases, the level of hatred or despair, that would not appreciably increase the likelihood of finding the culprit in this area; hatred and despair do not commonly unbalance the mind if relief is in sight, and not distant.

By contrast, just as the very imminence of Henry Midden's

[1] Inspector Coggin had yet to learn that in the jargon of radio a program produced in a rented, private-enterprise studio is called "an outhouse production": when he first heard the term, his prairie soul shook with a wild surmise (was it, perhaps, a reading of the Catalogue, on location?); and when the term was explained to him by a secretary who was bilingual in English and Gobbledygook, he realised it's no longer true to say, "Scratch a Canadian and you'll find a farmer."

44

retirement weakened the case against the Program people, so it must be held to strengthen the possible case against the people in Administration. He was more likely to have been murdered by an administrator than by a producer, if one considered hatred as a motive, or revenge. But there was every possibility that he might have been murdered by a colleague who wanted his job. Inspector Coggin had run across cases of convenient death in industry: some of them were prosecutable, others not; but they all stemmed from fights over power, not over products, and they all involved men in whom the wish to dictate was of paramount importance, who could not attach value to the worth of the merchandise or the need of the customer. Such men were mercifully few. But they were much drawn to key jobs: pure administrators, who had never drawn a real artisan's breath in their lives. Jobs of that kind, for their kind, seemed to be proliferating these days, and Henry Midden's job seemed to be one of them: it consisted, so far as he could see, in running the people who ran the networks, who in turn ran the department heads who ran the producers who ran the artists who wrote and performed the programs; it seemed to be a long way from creative work. At such a distance, conceivably, power can become the only thing in sight. The inspector was not at all sure how far crown corporations might differ from private business in their internecine ruthlessness:[2] but he did know that certain temperaments can become quite unbalanced through ambition; and there was no reason to suppose that people of this temperament would not be found in broadcasting. As to the imminence of Henry Midden's retirement, that would not necessarily make an ambitious rival wait: when a in a low key. In Sergeant Sump's view, which the inspector en- senior job is opening up, there are bound to be many candi-

[2] The answer, in fact, was six of one and half a dozen of the other. Job security was rampant in the CBC: this allowed the decent men, on the one hand, to go on being decent men without undue fear for their future; on the other hand, though, it allowed the unscrupulous free rein for their proclivities, because no offense they could commit (except theft) was known to get them fired.

dates; for any one of them, timing can be all-important. So the old question of motive still had value: Who stood to gain?

Now, however, was not the time or place to look into that; and anyway he was interrupted. "Come on," Michael Sherriff was exclaiming, "I'll show you the editing rooms." And he was threading his way, with practised alacrity, through the intricate defiles of tape and text.

Inspector Coggin followed, with some care for his shins, and contrived to emerge dislodging no more than the title page from the top script of the seventh pile on the left. It fluttered to the floor, a memento of his passing.

"Pneumatic Bliss," an Imaginary Conversation between T. S. Eliot and Mae West, written for radio by George Snipe.

Across the road, in the motel dining room, Miss Vulpitude was making slow work of a pork chop: the cuisine was adequate; but conversation kept getting in the way of ingestion. Sergeant Sump was well along with his cotelette de veau Bruno Simplex (veal cutlet with machismo sauce), and he, too, had ascertained that Henry Midden was due to retire soon. The likely candidates for his job, locally, were five: they were Midden's two immediate subordinates, who respectively had charge of the AM and FM networks; the head of the Department of Outside Broadcasts;[3] the Toronto assistant to the vice-president, Public Relations;[4] and the regional director of Opera-

---

[3] O.B. for short: a hold-all group, covering events of immense public importance like the Santa Claus Parade, purveying regularly the limp obligatory rhetoric of the Throne Speech, and occasionally transmitting dollops of documentary sound like Ben Thomson's renowned "Mating Calls of the Mackenzie Wagtail." Traditionally, heads of the department were promoted O.B. announcers, in whom sonority of utterance and glibness of phrase markedly outdistanced depth of intellect.

[4] P.R. work for the CBC was exceptionally difficult. It entailed a daily and seldom fruitful attempt to polish the corporation's image in a constantly hostile press. In addition, though, there was the extra and unwelcome burden of answering to the corporation's audiences: some viewers and listeners actually believed that the corporation's mandate was a valid yardstick for measuring its work, and they were tireless in their complaints. Their usual target, of course, was television, with its commercial slant and its extreme reliance on the shoddier American imports; but around this period these critics were also zeroing in on radio, on its belief that no

tions.[5] Between mouthfuls Miss Vulpitude, tactfully prompted
by Sergeant Sump, was giving short descriptions of each person.
She began by insisting that anything she said was, of course,
only one individual's opinion, and too much weight shouldn't
be attached to it. But as she continued, the necessity for this
disclaimer seemed to recede somewhat from her attention, and
she warmed to her task.

Lew Stukely, the director of the AM Network, was an intellectual snob—if that term can be held to connote someone
who looks down on tastes which differ from his own. In his
case, the dislike was for everything highbrow or lowbrow. He
was happy to leave all exacting music or serious ideas to the
FM Network, and all the self-evident garbage to the sleazier
private stations. His constituency, he felt, was the broad mass
of middle-class Canadians who liked background music, unpro-
tracted news bulletins, generous helpings of the high-profile
professional sports, and gossip. These were, in fact, his own
tastes: he had rationalized them into a policy. Asked to

---

one of taste or education lived in rural areas, and on its policy of abolishing
distinct programs and bundling various vaguely related items together in
long amorphous blocks of air time. The local man in charge of P.R. was
well suited to his post, in that the cult of mediocrity was, with him, a
passionately held creed: this meant that he was very supportive of safe
programs which avoided controversy and kept within the genteelest
bounds of good taste; he was also very adroit at fielding awkward questions and supplying suave responses which seemed to reply to them but
which turned out, on later reflection, to be almost entirely devoid of relevant content.

[5] An umbrella job: under it were assembled the various specialized departments each of which served all the program areas; for instance, the
libraries, the scheduling offices, the engineering section, and even the
cleaning staff. The ramifications of the job were enormous, and it was
never occupied by a specialist in one of its disciplines, but always by executives trained in pure managerial technique: this guaranteed its occupancy
by faceless men undevoted to causes; but it did have the corollary virtue
of ensuring impartiality. In recent years it so happened, through no deliberate policy, that the post had been held alternately by different types:
by conscientious men, who were rapidly driven to ulcers by the problems
of running a cumbersome plant on a minuscule budget; and by cynics, who
delegated most of their authority to specialized subordinates, on whom
they placed the blame for all botched work, but for whose successes they
themselves took all the credit. The current occupant was of the latter type.

describe how she viewed this, Miss Vulpitude said, "Well, I guess what they'd really like is to turn the corporation into a network version of CFRB—at the taxpayer's expense."[6]

Nobody seemed to know, she went on, why or how Joyce Parchment had become director of the FM Network. She was a middle-aged career woman who had risen through the ranks of the Personnel Department by the simple process of sticking around and being available for promotion when vacancies occurred. But it was a surprise to everyone when she was moved, a year ago, into her present post: for she had no perceptible qualifications for the job; and at least a token appearance of suitability would normally be required, if only to placate the disappointed. "But then tokenism, of a sort, was involved perhaps," Miss Vulpitude commented. "At least, you could say so. Because the corporation badly needed to have a woman in a senior post. Maybe she was the answer. She satisfied the demand without being likely to do too much damage. You see, one thing Mr. Midden liked was to keep the program areas well under his thumb. So having someone fairly biddable heading a network made that easier for him. I suppose that sounds rather catty. But I think, if they'd really tried, they could have found plenty of women who'd have been stronger and just generally more appropriate than Mrs. Parchment.[7] She isn't exactly a force to be reckoned with."

Bud Benedict,[8] the head of Outside Broadcasts, was younger,

[6] CFRB were the call-letters of a private station in Toronto which had had, over the years, enormous success in the ratings by applying to broadcasting the pragmatic dogma espoused in politics by the Liberal Party: that is, cover enough of the middle and you can ignore the fringes.

[7] After her divorce, twenty years ago, Joyce Parchment had retained her married surname, for the sake of her daughter, but had changed her appellation from Mrs. to Miss. Recently, when the vogue for that curious monosyllable came in, she had shortened this to Ms. However, Betsy Vulpitude, who had her own views on the lady and her life style, persistently addressed her as Mrs., greatly to her annoyance.

[8] Known to his French colleagues as Bébé le Moco because of his private predilection for sailors; and to his English colleagues as the BB-gun because of his public tendency to shoot off his mouth, without discernible effect.

48

at forty-three, than most executives of the same rank. His CBC career had been entirely in the one department, but he had risen by ups and downs rather than by steady advancement. Eighteen years ago, as a disc jockey on a middle-of-the-road private station, he had acquired the knack of speaking at some length off the top of his head[9] without saying anything. This had made him a useful recruit to O.B. during a time when most announcers were more interested in getting their faces seen on television than they were in serving radio's need for a mouthpiece on ceremonial or social or even agricultural occasions. He had quickly prospered. Few rivals could match the hushed and reverent manner with which he described the elevation of "Elbows" McSlaughter to the Hockey Hall of Fame, or the stolid flow of banalities with which he filled in when the Duchess of Uppingham failed to show for the annual tea-and-crumpets gala of the I.O.D.E., or the unyielding zest with which he rhapsodised over the centennial year Turnip Festival in Buttock, P.E.I. However, his promising future began to bog down, increasingly, in a proneness to alcohol. This reached the point where he had to be taken off the air: an occasional fuzziness of speech and a shaky grasp of facts had been forgiven him; but it was plain that he could not continue *in situ* after he'd addressed the then Governor-General, coast-to-coast, as "Roly, old boy." Ordinarily, he would have been shunted sideways, to a behind-the-scenes position where he could fuddle along without being in public view, enjoying some meaningless title like Program Development Consultant. That did not happen, though: for in that particular period the corporation had a personnel officer who had read up on the latest approach to industrial alcoholism; this has it that alcoholics should not be coddled with sick leave and sympathy, but rather should be threatened with dismissal and told that successful therapy is a condition of their continued employment. Accordingly, Bud Benedict had been forced into therapy and had quit drinking—

[9] A spot situated exactly six feet above ground level. The three inches below it were said by some to be a vacant space.

fear apparently being, in his case, a persuasive catalyst. About eight months later the head of O.B. transferred to television and Benedict was given his job, perhaps in part as a reward for his sobriety. If that had been a reason, it misfired: carrying out assignments, he had been loaded with self-confidence (even when loaded); supervising them, he was a bundle of insecurity, and in a few weeks he began to drink again, though only in the evenings. This renewed intemperance could not be hidden: he contrived to stay away from the booze all day, even at lunchtime, but he used to come in in the mornings with a shocking hangover; and this inevitably was noticed. However, the personnel officer who had handled his case had now departed to greener paydays in private industry; and before his successor could come to grips with the crisis, Benedict solved the problem by having a coronary. It was not a massive one, but there is no such thing as an unserious heart attack. When he was sufficiently recovered to leave hospital, his doctor told him that any further drinking would probably be fatal. This ultimate fear proved lastingly effective: he quit his therapist, whose success rate anyway (like that of his colleagues) was low enough to be described as fortuitous; and he joined AA, who succeeded with him as they have with countless others.[10] A beneficial side effect was the allaying, to some extent, of his anxieties. This helped him to handle his work more smoothly, and this improvement was compounded by the helpfulness of his colleagues: businessmen tend to go out of their way to give aid and comfort to any one of their number who has had a coronary and come back on the job; it is as though they saw

[10] The comparison is interesting: AA relies, pragmatically, on procedures which have been shown to work, without much bothering over why they work; psychotherapists, on the other hand, meddle with the human mind in a manner at once doctrinaire and experimental, meanwhile claiming for their ministrations the status of a science—clearly, they are uninstructed in what constitutes the scientific method. This disaster area lies outside the scope of the present report. But some day, no doubt, it will find its just satirists. We must hope that when they appear, they will employ, not the gentle humour of a de Maupassant or the crisp wit of a Waugh, but the denunciatory ridicule of a Juvenal. Quacks merit rhubarbs.

the writing on their own office wall. So, in his recent post-coronary years, Bud Benedict had flourished. He had not, of course, inaugurated any new policies in his department, for it was not in his nature to innovate or to create: as before, he still presented to a stupefied public a glutinous continuum of documentaries about spinach, coverage of admission rituals in the Canadian Senate, and reports from the annual general meeting of the Morticians Association in Hunter's Canal, Ontario; it was his tradition, and he maintained it. But at least he did maintain it. In an epoch when radio drama was being dramatically crippled and serious music seriously malhandled, O.B. had held its ground: not because its work was any good; but because no one was willing to take the responsibility for handing Bud Benedict a setback. This gave him an importance out of all proportion to the intrinsic worth of his programs or their value to his audiences, and he was commonly regarded as a coming man. He would not rank highly in the betting for Henry Midden's job, for it seemed more likely to most people that Lew Stukely would move up and be replaced by Benedict than that Benedict should leapfrog over Stukely. However, Miss Vulpitude had a rider to add to that. "You have to remember," she said, "the president used to have the same problem. He's been on the wagon for nearly thirty years now, but it's still a factor. You know how important solidarity is to reformed drunks. So you can't be too sure. It's just possible he might tap Mr. Benedict for the job after all." She finished her chop, and ordered blueberry pie.

"Now Arnold Gloss," she went on as she waited for it, "he's really something else. I don't think I care too much for P.R. men. They're too glib. Like salesmen. But this one certainly knows his job. You wait till you see him in action on today's doings. He'll have us coming up roses if anyone can. First of all, there'll be an eloquent tribute to Mr. Midden as a man and a leader of men (have you ever noticed, Sergeant, how these conventional phrases omit any reference to women?): just sufficient time will be spent on his long years with the corporation and his services to broadcasting; then that part of it will be wrapped up with an allusion to the affection and esteem in which he was held by all his colleagues."

She took a sip of her 2 per cent milk and continued. "Next, I should imagine Mr. Gloss will make some mention of yourself and the inspector, and will say we all feel the matter's in good hands and all hope for a speedy solution of it. Meanwhile (and here he will become very firm and solemn) everyone present will surely agree that it's our duty to the deceased to carry on his work: fortunately, he had the good of the corporation ever at heart and his plans for the coming months were well in hand; the corporation will weather this sad crisis as it has weathered others in the past not of its own making—above all, we must realise that Henry Midden was the kind of pro for whom it was always true that The Show Must Go On: he would have wanted us to remember that today. At this point there will be a distinct catch in Mr. Gloss's voice, and he will just add, with a quiet note of sincerity, 'Thank you, I think that's all,' and sit down."

The blueberry pie arrived, and Miss Vulpitude contemplated it, her fork poised over it like a spearfisher's spear caught in a stillness of concentration above some especially elusive specimen. Then she struck: "What distresses me about all that," she said, "is it's all a pack of lies."

While Sergeant Sump munched away on a discouraging lump of starch libellously described as Meringue Napoléon à la Jehane Benoit, Miss Vulpitude pursued her point, with intermittent pauses for pie. She was far too well-mannered to come right out and say that Henry Midden was disliked and feared by everyone under or around him, including Arnold Gloss. But this was clearly implied. For she strongly deprecated the custom of eulogies. "I don't know which I dislike more," she concluded: "a flowery funeral speech by a minister who never met the deceased, or a glowing obituary of someone thoroughly unlikeable; but I do know they're both hypocritical, and if there's one thing I can't stand it's that."

She stabbed her last piece of pie, and Sergeant Sump wasn't

sure if this was mere emphasis or perhaps the expression of
some private grudge or unpleasant recollection; we've all been
through a bad funeral at some time in our lives, he reflected;
maybe she has recently. "After all," Miss Vulpitude added, "a
person may have been pretty worthless in his life. But he was a
human being, and that makes him worth *something*. So if you
can't think of anything good to say and mean it, then don't say
anything. Being lied about's no way to go. No one's bad
enough to deserve that."

There was a pause while coffee was served. Then the conversation brightened as Miss Vulpitude came on to the last of the
five people under discussion: Norm Casement, the Regional
Director of Operations. "The nice thing about Norm," she
said, "is that with him you know exactly where you stand.
Chances are he'll have your grandmother fried, for breakfast;
but at least he'll tell you he's going to."

Sergeant Sump winced, recollecting the type she referred to.
Some years ago, he had been working in the Brandon area and
had been assigned to help the Military Police investigate a
murder in the camp. The victim was a provost sergeant who,
by all accounts, had been an atrocious bully: ever vigilant for
the least offence against regulations—even for trifling and acci-
dental infringements of the dress regulations, for instance—he
arrested all offenders with the maximum physical force permitted, pressed against them the strongest possible charges, and
did everything he could to see that the most stringent penalties
were inflicted. He was entirely open about this, and indeed
used to warn new arrivals, "I'm a hard man, so keep your noses
clean if you know what's good for you." Draconic justice un-
touched by mercy was justified, in his eyes, by the fact that he
never overstepped the legal bounds of what was allowed to
him; he greatly enjoyed the fear which he engendered. One
morning his body was found behind the guardhouse. He had
been kicked to death. The entire body was one mass of kick
marks, suggesting the work of several assailants. News of his
fate had spread instantly throughout the camp. By the time the
investigation began, every soldier in the place had thoroughly

scrubbed, cleaned, and polished his boots to an identical state of glossy innocence which totally stymied the criminological lab. And their testimony was, in fact, a unanimous conspiracy of silence. The case was never solved.[11] Recalling it now, Sergeant Sump winced, not because the case had been one of his few failures: rather, because it disquieted him to think that a bunch of average, ordinarily decent men could be driven to such lengths, and because, too, it went against the grain of his training to feel strong sympathy for the killers and no sorrow for the victim.

Norm Casement, Miss Vulpitude was saying, had always been a hard man to get along with, and knew it, and was unashamed. Superficially, his manner was cordial, not to say hearty. But the style was at variance with the content, which was at once tyrannous and insensitive. In brief, the man was an ogre. He steamrolled through life, crushing whatever lay in his path, all the while doing so with a flow of joviality which served the same end as everything else he did: to overpower. At meetings he was notorious: in support of ideas, especially his own, he would simply wear the opposition down, loudly, like a rhinoceros unstopped by the flimsy darts of pygmies; with ideas he objected to, he was a one-man demolition squad, and the only disagreement about his technique concerned merely whether his rudeness was calculated or spontaneous. Miss Vulpitude averred that never in recent years had the librarians and the engineers been kept better in line—or contributed less to broadcasting. Obedience was tops, morale at an all-time low.

"But why do you think he's in line for Mr. Midden's job?" Sergeant Sump asked. "Surely no corporation in its right mind would put a man like that in charge of a key area like the whole of radio."

Miss Vulpitude made no comment on whether or not the CBC might be in its right mind: she was more interested in in-

[11] Readers with a knowledge of Canadian military history will notice a curious resemblance between this case and one which occurred in Halifax in 1945.

dividual situations than general ironies. "Two reasons," she replied. "First, he's not like your average head of a single department: he has several departments under him, in what amounts to a small empire; and small emperors usually like to acquire bigger empires. So I figure he wants the job. And what Norm Casement wants, he usually gets." She took a gulp of the tan sludge which passed for coffee, and resumed. "The second reason's a bit more complicated. Right now management's having a lot of trouble with the producers. They're demanding a much bigger say in program planning and decision making. Just generally being a lot more uppity than they used to. Needless to say, management isn't about to cave in. But unfortunately things have come to a point where the two sides seem to be polarized. Looks like there'll have to be a showdown. If there is, management'll win it. They have too many cards in their hand. But, of course, they want to be sure. So having someone like Norm Casement in charge would really suit them very well. He could be counted on not to stand any nonsense, and I don't know that the producers would have any answers for a general manager who treated them like sewer workers." The allusion seemed to remind Miss Vulpitude of her coffee: she pushed the half-finished cup ruefully aside. "Of course," she concluded, "that's only what I think personally. Officially, I'm not supposed to have any opinions."

Sergeant Sump thanked her for all she had told him, called for the bill, and paid it out of expenses. The amount was fairly substantial, but he considered the taxpayer's money well spent, in view of all he'd been told. His one regret was that the profit would go to an outfit whose version of food closely resembled the modern version of hockey: tasteless and unskilled.

At the next table a television executive was paying a somewhat larger bill, also at the taxpayer's expense, for a lunch (consisting largely of alcohol) with a writer, in the course of which they had discussed gay liberation at some length and, for five minutes, a book the guest was hoping to write which might one day perhaps have a fugitive relevance to a possible pilot program. It was also considered, by the host, to be money well spent.

"Years ago," Michael Sherriff had said to Inspector Coggin in the staff cafeteria, "when I was new here and didn't know any better, I had one of their cooked lunches. Shepherd's pie. It took a while before I was served, and I fell into a brown study. A couple of minutes later I was jolted back to reality by having a plate thrust into my hand containing what I can only describe as mashed potatoes and boiled mucus, both of them grey. Simultaneously, a comment from just behind me: Frank Geddes, who was a marvellous old actor from Scotland, was next to me in the line-up; and he looked at the plate I was holding, and said 'Ye ken, I a'ways wondered what happened to auld shepherds when they dee'd.' "

The inspector had avoided the cooked lunches. A line from Malory flitted through his head: "And but we avoid wisely, there is but death." He settled for toast, a banana, and a tin of tomato juice.

"Mind you," Sherriff had gone on, "that was several managements ago: they let the franchise out on tender from time to time, and the present company's a good deal more reliable." He picked out a salad, a yogurt, and a carton of milk. "But the place which has really got it to rights is the radio station in West Berlin: they have two staff cafeterias, and they let the franchises out to two different companies; so they have to compete with each other in quality and price. Smart fellows, those Germans."

They had threaded their way through the sparse agglomeration of lunchers to one of several empty tables. And while they ate, Sheriff had held forth on interoffice politics, on tape-editing, on audience research, and exhaustively on the stupidity of the senior executive who had abolished the CBC Times. Inspector Coggin had listened attentively but with a certain impatience: he was eager to get back to the Administration Building. There was something important he wanted to ask Miss Vulpitude.

FOUR

Tuesday, 1:00–2:00

PROGRAM SCHEDULE ⚡3: *Tuesday 1:00–2:00*

1:00　News

1:15　"Siesta": music for relaxing. Today, from the Islets of Langherhans, B.C., relax with Pierce Grieve and his orchestra, featuring the songs of Salmonella Pitts.

1:00　"Matinee," a series of experimental scripts for radio: this week, *Tarzan Agonistes* by Marguerite Dubois, a verse-portrait of Albrecht Berthold, the Berlin monkey-fucker; starring Roger Gibbons, with incidental music by Simeon Cage, and directed by Aimée Cousins.

1:30　"Contemporary Recital," music of today performed by Canadian artists (repeat of program from last Friday evening): *Blbosti* by Zilkmund Švestka-Indra, for quislinghorn and Russian contraphone, played by Agatha Parrott and Leonid Smašček. *Séparations Aléatoriques* by Désirée Lachance, for orator and turned percussion caps, spoken by René Cardinal and detonated by F. L. Curie; text by Charles de Gaulle. *Etwas* by Karlheinz Niemand for variable consort, played by the Gastown Wind Septet and Cosmo Omnivast, synthesizer.

"MISS VULPITUDE," Inspector Coggin said, "I want you to tell me everything you can about Mr. Midden's use of his dictaphone. And also how you yourself worked with it after he'd used it. First of all, for instance, did he use it a lot?"

"Yes, quite frequently." Miss Vulpitude cast her mind back to her many sessions with it. That harsh, unmistakable voice had poured into her ear almost daily a series of memos, letters, and instructions; few of them were pleasant, most of them were astute, all of them were ungrammatical. It was strange to think she would never have to transcribe (and correct) them again. "He preferred it to dictating in person. Figured I could get on with other things while he dictated to the machine. I guess he was right at that. But it was a bit ironic: most girls nowadays can't take dictation, except slowly, with what they call Speedwriting; whereas my shorthand is actually quite good, if he'd wanted to rely on it. Oh well, maybe the next man . . ."

Inspector Coggin steered her back to the point. "Fine. So he used it frequently. And how did you organize your work with it? Was there any fixed pattern?"

"I can't say I've ever given it much thought, Inspector. But he'd usually ask me to transcribe it right away if it was urgent. And if not I'd start in on it whenever it was convenient. Usually, I'd try and get it all done by quitting time, but naturally I couldn't if he'd dictated a large amount at the very end of the afternoon: then it would have to wait till next day."

"And what did he do when he wanted to start a new batch of dictation? Did he just put in a new reel and fire away? Or did you load it for him, or what?"

"It was always loaded." Miss Vulpitude was quite firm about anything that concerned her professional competence. "Any time I took a reel away for transcribing, I automatically replaced it with a fresh one. And I always did that at the end of the day: if there was anything on the reel, I took it out and replaced it with a fresh one, so the machine would be ready for him to use if he came in early (he used to sometimes, you know); and anyway there's bound to be the odd morning when I'm late in myself." Even Miss Vulpitude, it seemed, partook of human frailty. Or did she? The seeming concession was deftly redirected. "I have to come in by the parkway. Your colleagues really ought to do something about that situation, Inspector."

"Believe me, they'd like to. But I'm afraid the situation won't improve much so long as we have a city council which thinks the automobile will go away if you sufficiently frustrate its driver." Inspector Coggin checked himself before launching on one of his pet themes, the probability that car drivers would one day sufficiently unite to be able to elect a slate of genuine reform candidates, to replace the present agglomeration of Neanderthal ward heelers and adolescent pseudo-reformists. This near-lapse into relaxed irrelevancy was a measure of the extent to which he was beginning to trust Miss Vulpitude. He sighed: trust is a luxury which police officers, on the job, cannot afford. He resumed his enquiries. "Did you clear the machine last night before going home?"

"I think the word I used, Inspector, was *always*. Last night was no exception."

Within, despite the reproof, Inspector Coggin cheered. Here was a witness who valued exactness. They were not common. "So when you went home, to the best of your knowledge, there was a blank tape on the machine? And the recording I found on the tape this morning must have been made since five o'clock last night?"

"Yes. Three minutes past five, if you want to be precise."

Precision was definitely what Inspector Coggin did want. "In your experience," he went on, "did Mr. Midden take the dictaphone home with him?"

"No. Never."

"And had he already left for the day when you went home?"

"Yes and no." Miss Vulpitude explained herself: "He'd left the office, but he wasn't going home: he had an eight o'clock meeting, and he was going to eat downtown."

"So let me get this straight, Miss Vulpitude. He could have come back here before that meeting or stayed on after it, or he could have come in early this morning. But the recording must have been made somewhere in that time span; and if he stuck to his usual pattern, he'll have made it here. Is that right?"

"Yes."

"Good. That's very helpful, thanks a lot. Oh, by the way, who was the meeting with?"

"Some of the other brass." Miss Vulpitude used the word *brass* nonchalantly and without colour, as a farmer might the word *dung*. "The Canada Youth Festival's coming up in the fall, and we have to decide what kind of special coverage to give it. So Mr. Midden asked me to set up a meeting with the two network bosses and the head of Outside Broadcasts; plus, of course, our operations chief and the publicity director. They were all too busy to get together in office hours."

"I see." Inspector Coggin turned to go on in to the inner office where Henry Midden had worked, and where he and Sergeant Sump would now conduct their interviews. He paused. "I think that'll be all just now, Miss Vulpitude. But I would be grateful if you'd stick around and handle all the CBC calls that come in. I'm sure you'll know how to take care of them. And if there are any calls for me, perhaps you'll get on the intercom and let me know who it is. Does it work, by the way? Mr. Sherriff seems to have been having some difficulty with his."

Miss Vulpitude smiled. She knew exactly what he was alluding to. "In Administration," she said, "the intercom always works."

He went about his business.

In the inner office, Sergeant Sump was waiting for him with an account of his luncheon conversation with Miss Vulpitude. Also waiting was the police typist with the transcript of the tape in Henry Midden's dictaphone. The sergeant had already read it, and listened to the tape. Inspector Coggin read the transcript. It was a top-secret memo to the president.

"As you know," it began, "I am due to retire in the early part of next year. It would be most improper of me to try and influence in any way your decision as to the choice of my successor. I am confident that you will give all possible candidates a thorough review, and that when you have done so you will make the best choice among them.

"However, since such a review is so important, it would also be most improper for me to withhold from you any information you might need, some of which perhaps only I could provide. Accordingly, I intend in this memo to lay before you some highly confidential information about some of the possible candidates. You will, of course, decide for yourself what value, if any, it may have to you in your ponderings. I ask only that you regard this information as something strictly between you and me, and that you not divulge the source of it."

Not bad as the prelude to a hatchet job, Inspector Coggin reflected. Henry Midden may have been one ripe bastard, and by all accounts thus far he was; but he certainly knew how to set things up his own way.

The next paragraph lumped together all the out-of-town candidates in one brisk conspectus, paid graceful tribute to their

63

abilities, and dismissed them out of hand. "I am sure you will agree that our new buildings in Montreal and Vancouver have done quite enough for the present to assuage the Westmount paranoids and the B.C. separatists; and that candidates from smaller centres simply do not have the background to handle responsibilities of the size you have in recent years entrusted to me. By contrast, there are several candidates in this region who have had plenty of insight into those responsibilities, and I do not doubt it is they whom you'll chiefly be scrutinizing. After all, Toronto *is* the nerve centre of our operation, and it would be idle to deny this."

Inspector Coggin scribbled out the names and locations of the out-of-town candidates, handed it to Sergeant Sump, and asked him to get the respective forces started on making checks: it would be necessary to know if any of these people could have been in Toronto last night.

The memo next listed the five local people who were likely candidates. It was the same list as Miss Vulpitude had given to Sergeant Sump over lunch. He noted this coincidence of opinion, decided to give it as yet no interpretation, and read on. The four men were dealt with first, all in the same way. Each was given a paragraph in which, to begin with, his ability and his suitability were acknowledged; then, in closing, each had the rug pulled out from under him. These four shafting conclusions read as follows:

Lew Stukely: "You will recall our deep embarrassment of a few years ago, when it became necessary to plant an RCMP officer in our midst (ostensibly as a Dr. Atisbar from the Harvard Business School, on a visit to study our management methods) in order to investigate kickbacks allegedly paid by CBC artists. No conclusive evidence was ever found which could properly form the basis either of dismissal or of court action. But I must tell you that very grave suspicions were aroused about the activities of one man, and one man only. Since these suspicions did not constitute proof, it was not possible to take the matter any further. But it would be wrong of me now not to tell you that that man was Lew Stukely."

Bud Benedict: "It has been said, at a rather august level, that governments have no business in the bedrooms of the nation. Perhaps this is also true of CBC administrations. But I do not think you will want to appoint as general manager a closet queen. Such persons are nowadays less liable to blackmail than formerly, since there is more public tolerance of their perversion; so anxiety on those grounds perhaps need not be a bar to promotion. However, real anxiety on another score must, I believe, stand in the way. I refer to the fact that queers hire queers. Once you let one in at the top, the whole apparatus is quickly penetrated by others (if you'll pardon the expression); and one thing the CBC can definitely not afford at this stage of its history is the allegation, especially a well-founded allegation, that it has become a breeding ground for pansies. I am sorry to have to tell you that this objection applies, without doubt, to Bud Benedict."

Arnold Gloss: "You may well think that someone with his special attainments would be just the man we need in the next few years. Anyone who can improve the corporation's image, with government or the public and especially with the press, must seem attractive at a time when we are so much under attack. And image-polishing is definitely his forte. However, nothing is more destructive of efforts in this direction than discernible insincerity. And I'm afraid that Arnold Gloss regards his job of 'selling' the CBC as strictly a nine-to-five proposition. After hours, he has been known to employ terms which, to say the least, fall short of adulation: our latest program schedule, for instance, was described as 'a pile of crap'; and I'm sorry to say that he's referred to the president's office as 'a home for ex-lushes who couldn't find work.' You will doubtless agree that this tendency of his would make him a poor risk."

Norm Casement: "Some people seem to think his blend of aggressiveness and stubbornness would be very useful to us in any future showdown with the producers. Personally, I cannot agree. Norm, for all his sterling qualities, is the last person to deal effectively with the kind of dissidence we may have to face: he's too unyielding; it does not occur to him that in order to win a campaign you may have to lose a few skirmishes. A less abrasive personality would use quite other methods to keep these people in their place: the secret of success, probably, is to appear to endorse their policy while not in fact adopting their platform; but this technique would be quite beyond Norm. An example of his inflexibility was his recent scotching of the plan to renovate our studios: it's quite true, of course, that there was also much value in the alternative plan he supported, to hire section aides to all executive assistants attached to officers of rank 5 or above; but this could perhaps have waited a year or two, and meanwhile he succeeded in alienating not only all of the producers and engineers but also yourself, I imagine, since the renovation plan had originated with you."

So much for the last two, thought Inspector Coggin: only a president of great magnanimity would discount attacks upon his character or subversion of his projects; men in such positions were more known for ego than for magnanimity. He remembered, ruefully, the definition of a good chief executive: "Someone who hires people smarter than himself"—ruefully, because the definition could not, in recent years, have described anyone at the top level of the police department.

As to the first two, it was a neat job of character assassination. The charge of being a closet queen, for instance, was almost impossible to disprove: the taint would stick, even if there was no evidence. And the charge of taking kickbacks was equally insidious: it might or might not be true that Stukely had been the prime suspect (a quick check with the RCMP would sort that out), but Midden was unlikely to have risked alleging it if it wasn't true; and so, however immoral it might be to defame a man on mere suspicion and without proof, the damage was done, irreparably.

He paused for a minute to consider the flavour of this memo. Seldom, it seemed to him, had he come across such an extraordinary combination of grasp, grasp of a large situation, and petty-mindedness, the petty-minded malice of the emotionally stunted. He recognised the latter trait well enough: in his

66

younger years, on the beat, he'd encountered it often in adolescent punks who did wanton damage to property or mindless hurt to people, for no reason other than spiteful whim. But he had not expected to encounter the trait in a senior officer of the CBC: not having listened to its programs for some years, he still associated that body with classical music, literate news, and high-minded opinions. He read on.

"The fifth candidate with real qualifications is obviously Joyce Parchment. During this past year, I have found her support invaluable as Director of the FM Network; and I am sure you are aware of how well she has acquitted herself in that demanding position. There is, however, one especially attractive talent of hers which you may be unaware of. I refer to her extraordinary capacity for nullifying any criticism or resistance, either laterally or from below. In this she is the exact opposite of Norm Casement. Her immediate response, when faced with such problems, is a disarmingly sympathetic attention: she takes the issue under review, whatever it may be, to be dealt with at the appropriate time in the appropriate way; but then, as it turns out, the appropriate time never arrives, and the issue disappears out of sheer inertia. I cannot tell you how helpful this has been to me: time and time again in recent months, we have been plagued by mouthy radicals in Production, who seem to think the tail should wag the dog; and every time, they have retired baffled. It could be said that this ability of Ms. Parchment's constitutes her one resemblance to a brick wall—something to hit your head against to no good effect."

That last touch, Inspector Coggin thought, was a real clue to character. Most people would have finished the sentence at "brick wall." Midden felt impelled to go on, to explain the obvious. Insensitivity of that kind is not the mark of a pleasing character.

"I need hardly add," Midden had concluded, adding it anyway, "that if you were indeed to promote her to general manager, the appointment would have the merit of being absolutely noncontroversial. In the atmosphere of today, it is hard to imagine anyone having the temerity to deprecate the choice of a woman: everyone would have to fall into line. That is doubtless a consideration at a time when unity of purpose will be so important to our future.

"The securing of that future, my dear President, is of course what has prompted me to write this memo. The ball is now, as they say, in your court. If you have found these remarks unhelpful, you can totally ignore them. And even if they should prove to some extent useful to you, that, too, is entirely your own concern from here on in. I do not expect, or wish, to be consulted about the matter at all.

"As always, with kindest regards,
Henry Midden."

Well, that last expectation was more on target than he could have known, the inspector mused: Henry Midden hadn't even lived to sign his name. He laid the transcript down on the dead man's desk. "Well, Fred," he asked, "what do you make of it?"

Sergeant Sump grinned wryly. "And we thought we had it bad in the Department," he said. "Well, at least we've never had to work for a bastard like *that*. One thing crossed my mind, though. How sure can we be that Miss Vulpitude hasn't heard that tape? We've only her word for it that it wasn't dictated until some time last night. And for that matter she may even have listened to it this morning before we arrived. But there's certainly a lot in that memo that parallels what she was telling me at lunch. Mind you, that could be perfectly innocent coincidence. Or maybe everyone around here would come out with the same line of thought, if asked. Then again, even if she *has* heard the tape, it doesn't follow she's implicated in anything criminal: she may simply have been unable to resist the temptation to show off her knowledge of top-level shenanigans; I can imagine that working for Henry Midden over any length of time would build up a pretty sizeable head of frustration."

"Yes, we'll just have to keep an open mind on that for the present," the inspector agreed. "It may mean something. It may not. Personally, my instinct is to trust her: it was probably

just coincidence. But we don't have to back any one interpretation yet." He took up another point. "You know what
struck me, Fred? This Joyce Parchment must be quite some
woman if Midden was prepared to go to such lengths to push
her candidacy and kill off everyone else's chances. It's a good
job I'm a happily married man."

Sergeant Sump sighed: the inspector, like most intellectuals,
was an incurable romantic; given the possibility that a case contained a femme fatale, he invariably expected a beauty of out-
rageous magnetism—he never seemed to learn that it is the unexpectedly plain-looking woman, as often as not, who has men
grovelling in the clutches of some inexplicable sexual domina-
tion.

These ruminations were interrupted by the inspector. He was
listening to the first part of the tape again and timing it on his
wristwatch. "I've decided we have to at least trust Miss Vulpitude this much," he said: "she's the only person qualified to
identify his voice as it sounded on the dictaphone. If she
hasn't, in fact, heard the tape, there are things on it she
shouldn't hear. But there won't be any harm in playing her the
first two paragraphs—I've timed them and I'll know when to
stop. That should be enough for her to verify if it's really
Henry Midden's voice or not. I imagine it is. There may be
some pretty good voice imitators among the radio actors. But I
doubt if they'd be good enough to fool a man's personal secretary."

"Unless, of course, she was in on it," Sergeant Sump reminded him.

"Well, yes, there's always that," the inspector conceded.
"But even if she was, there's nothing to lose by asking her. It
just means we can't take her answer at a hundred per cent face
value." He called her in and explained what he wanted her to
do. She sat down and put the earphone in her ear. He started
the tape.

After three sentences Miss Vulpitude motioned to him to
stop. "Oh yes," she said, "that's Mr. Midden's voice all right.

69

No doubt about it." The two men watching her concluded she was either completely candid or else a consummate actress: for as soon as she heard the playback, her face had registered immediate recognition, followed by an obvious discomfort at hearing so palpably alive the voice of a man so newly dead. She looked up, "Perhaps I ought to hear a little more, though," she said, "just to be absolutely sure."

Inspector Coggin glanced at his watch, played her the second paragraph, and then pushed the stop button. She took the earphone off and put it down reflectively. "No, there isn't any doubt. That's him." She paused. "Was there anything else, Inspector?"

"No, not just now, thank you, Miss Vulpitude."

She got up and left the room with a faint air of dissatisfaction (which did not elude the notice of Sergeant Sump). There was something about that tape that bothered her. It was Henry Midden's voice beyond question. And yet something was there which didn't seem quite right. Whatever was it? For a moment she toyed with the idea that perhaps Mr. Midden had dictated the memo under duress and that this had affected his manner, but then "Don't be melodramatic, Betsy," she told herself: "this isn't a television crime show." But then again, she reflected, murder, by its very nature, is melodramatic. Maybe it would come to her, whatever had been wrong with what she'd heard. But it bothered her not to be able to spot what it was.

FIVE

Tuesday, 2:00–2:30

PROGRAM SCHEDULE #4: *Tuesday 2:00–2:30*

2:00 News

2:04 National Schools Program: Grade 10, Canadian Studies: "Albert Sneed: founder of Axilla, New Brunswick; poet-telegrapher; and inventor of the side-angled rotary onion-trimmer." Script, Alf Hackney. Production, Hilda Cleat.

2:00 "Collage," a daily compendium of recorded music and the spoken word, for discriminating listeners. The first part of this afternoon's program will include "Postlude à l'après-midi d'un satyr" by Pierre de Saint-Pussy; "Daphne and Chloë," a selection from the love sonnets of Victoria Dyke; and "Opus for Organ" by Rod Taylor.

Fʀᴇᴅ Sᴜᴍᴘ ᴡᴀs a collector of words: words as a key to character, not as things valuable in themselves. He liked listening to people, and had a knack of hearing behind the words whatever was left unsaid, by the afraid or the inarticulate or the guilty. And he wasn't often wrong about guilt: most of us blush and stammer at the mere possibility of blame for wrongs we haven't committed; but he knew this differed from the real miscreant's response, the sudden shift in the focus of the eyes, and then, in the unhesitating utterance of the smooth, plausible lies, a just perceptibly extra attention to their effect, the same kind of attentiveness a violinist gives to the nuance of each note in a slow passage, however well rehearsed. These, to Sergeant Sump, were the two uses of language: to express and, by accident or design, to conceal: he relished both.

To Inspector Coggin, on the other hand, language was a tool. In the hands of a good writer, a precision tool. On the lips of most people, a blunt instrument: an offence against themselves, like the bulging gut and short wind of a man who pays no honour to his body. He was not a snob about this: formal prose was not to be expected in conversation, and he loved

74

good, lively slang; but neither virtue was found in the discourse
of most people. This had little to do with intelligence or education: often enough there was no lack of intelligence behind the
unsufficing words; and all too often, behind them, there stood a
college degree. But in either case, he felt, much more was involved than merely grammar or vocabulary: eventually the
crippling of the language must be attended by a crippling of
mind and morale; if everyone spoke of *inappropriate societal re-*
sponse, not of *selfishness*; of *unsublimated physical overreac-*
tion, not of *assault*; and of *questionable business practices*, not
of *theft*, then no one would think clearly about these things
any more, or abstain from them. He wasn't sure which was the
cause and which was the effect. But he was convinced of the
connection: crime flourished as language and accuracy decayed.

Listening to witnesses, then, they heard quite different
things. Sergeant Sump, while not ignoring matter, paid great
heed to manner: why did the lady with the emphatic lipstick
become edgy when asked about cucumbers; and did the little
aristocrat with the British accent abstain from deodorants as a
badge of his origin or was there perhaps some nasty individual
quirk involved. Inspector Coggin, on the other hand, while not
ignoring manner, paid great heed to matter: somewhere, he
reasoned, behind that clutter of maimed words there must be a
meaning trying to get out: stubbornly, he pieced it together;
but he couldn't help wincing when the high school English
teacher bleated *you know* eleven superfluous times in the
first two minutes. Broadcasters, he would soon discover, were
just as bad: evidently employment in communications was no
guarantee of lucid thoughts couched in clear words. He would
not be surprised by what passed for language among the CBC
bureaucrats, since this was indistinguishable from the slack-
minded dialect spoken in the upper reaches of policedom: but
he would never entirely shed the initial shock of realizing that
news bulletins could be written, at public expense and for public consumption, by people who didn't know that singular sub-
jects and plural verbs are a mismatch. By the time he died, he

75

often thought, English would be a dead language, superseded by reflex noises of pain or pleasure, refusal or consent, as imprecise and unexacting as the first grunts and groans in the ancestral cave. A fitting enough fate, other things considered. What else but vapidity of expression does any culture deserve which has given the world processed cheese, margarine, and taste-free bread?

What the two men had in common, in their taste for language, was the *Globe and Mail* crossword: the cryptic one, which flattered the solver's vanity by suggesting it would occupy his mind for forty minutes. They had both happened to hear one morning, with exactly equal astonishment, a radio interview with Ivan Coughlan, a Toronto alderman who cultivated a highly cerebral image, but who admitted, when asked, that this crossword usually took him the full forty minutes it claimed to need. Neither of them, as a rule, took longer than nine minutes to finish it: on a good day, each of them could break six minutes. Once in a while, of course, one of them would be stumped with one obdurate clue unsolved, to the great glee of his partner: for the same clue would almost never stump both of them; their methods and approaches were too different. Inspector Coggin was brilliant at the analytic problems: anagrams, manipulations of orthography, anything that smacked of code. Sergeant Sump, on the other hand, responded instantly to any flight of fancy: if the clue suggested an aural kinship between *rain* and *reign*, he was onto it at once, with a quick nod of agreement about the wetness of the monarchy before moving on to the next clue; the bizarre always pleased him, the appropriately bizarre delighted him.

This morning, however, was one of those rare occasions when the same clue had frustrated them both. Twenty across: "This orange is not ultra-marine, but sounds quasi-marine"; five letters. As such things go, it was, of course, relatively simple. But circumstances had prevented their giving it any more than cursory thought: Sergeant Sump's seventeen-year-old, Felicity, had cut short his last minutes at home after breakfast by unexpectedly needing a ride to school, having pulled a back muscle the night before at a drive-in (blurred recollections of his own adolescent gropings in the rear seat twenty-five years ago were adroitly snubbed by the information that what she'd been doing actually, Daddy, was helping change a flat tire—he felt a mild incestuous relief); and at about the same hour, Mrs. Coggin had asked the inspector if he could perhaps leave a couple of minutes early and return a borrowed wrench to her sister who needed it for a big plumbing job she was into, you know how useless John is at things like that, oh, and don't forget the Foots are coming to dinner (why not the Feet, he wondered—it's an odd language), so you'd better pick up some club soda on the way home, and maybe a raincoat would be a good idea after all, 'bye, dear, and have a nice day. Since then they'd both been too busy to pay any more attention to the crossword.

President Laval, in differing ways, was a pleasure to each of them: his use of language was, to Inspector Coggin, a pleasing thing in itself; to Sergeant Sump, it was a pleasantly intriguing clue to character.

English was not the president's mother tongue, and so he used it much more meticulously than is common among Anglos. He constructed sentences with a beginning, a middle, and an end, imposing on them often an almost Jamesian complexity in which he never lost his way, and using throughout correct grammar. He even remembered that "presently" does not mean "at present," and he avoided the current misuse of "hopefully" and of "disinterested." He knew when subjunctives were needed. Indeed, his only weak spot was his vocabulary: it was large and, for the most part, accurate; but every now and then an incorrect word would appear and puncture the illusion of total fluency. These misusages, usually, stemmed from a similarity to a French usage: he meant to say "attend" and would say "assist," or when he meant to say "wait" he would say "attend." Occasionally, too, he would make the mistake of literal translation: "elevating himself," for instance, in the morning.

Errors like this lent a beguiling flavour of risk to his prose: it was like watching a show-jumper negotiate a series of high fences and then trip over a twig.

"You can therefore imagine, can you not," he was saying, "how profoundly it would be to my wish that this homicide, if such indeed it be (and there would seem, alas, to be little doubt upon that score), should explain itself to be a willful, nay an arbitrary, occurrence visited upon our poor friend not only by the malign will of fate, but also by the hand of a total foreigner." Inspector Coggin found himself waiting for the lapses and counting them: guiltily he reminded himself that there ought to be a difference between the small boy watching the large man skid on a banana peel and a policeman listening to a public servant hoping to shield his corporate dignity.

Sergeant Sump, meanwhile, was weighing the man behind the words, seeking connections with the man he'd read up on in the file supplied by H.Q. His preliminary response had been to dismiss him as a pretentious bore who liked using fancy language. Then he caught an extra quality: the man was listening attentively to his own performance. This could have one or more of several meanings: vanity, the unspontaneity of using a second language, a desire to mislead or cajole, bad conscience; all these were possible. In a way, they all boiled down to self-protection. Sergeant Sump suspected that President Laval's anxiety that the CBC not be afflicted with scandal stemmed less from loyalty to the corporation than from concern for his own career: if the murder turned into a dirty-laundry-day for CBC management, the chief executive could hardly expect that when his stop-gap term was up he would be rewarded with some such plum as the ambassadorship to Monaco. And such expectations would be important to a man who had earned his appointment by selfless years as a bagman for the Quebec Liberals.

"A foreigner who simply walked in off the street," the president added. "It is, I believe, not unknown in the modern annals of violence, extensive as they are, for such an incident to unroll itself. One reads of ancient ladies assassinated for thirty-five cents; of shopping plazas terrorised by psychotic snipers; of innocents beaten beyond recognisance but at apparent random by drunk aggressors. These histories do little to allay (if anything, they confirm) our now almost pandemic fear for plain physical surety. But then, without doubt, you will have considered this already. It is not for me to teach you your affair."

"Thank you, yes, we did think of that," Inspector Coggin replied. "We will, of course, explore every avenue, that included. But it's only fair to tell you we think the other two possibilities more likely."

"To wit?"

Inspector Coggin had never before actually heard someone say "to wit": he added it to his personal collection of vintage clichés, along with "your very humble servant" (Rev. Angus Sporran, Cardiac Presbyterian Church, N.S., May 5, 1963) and "inasmuch as which" (Inez Moskovitz, M.P., House of Commons, October 16, 1952). "To wit," he replied, "deliberate murder by somebody who knew him in either his personal or his professional life."

"But that would be most distressing." In an injured tone, the president managed to imply that the police would somehow be obscurely at fault if this turned out to be the case, if they did not chide the truth into rearranging itself to spare him distress.

Sergeant Sump had seen this reaction before, often: the parents of the teen-age car thief asking themselves not where they had failed him, but what this would do to their reputation; the wife of the petty embezzler seeing herself, not the swindled, as victim; the father of the pregnant high-schooler impervious to blame when she died, rejected by him, on the abortionist's table. Always the self first. It was an unlovely human failing.

"Naturally," the president continued, "you must do whatever, in the interests of justice, you can, to lay the perpetrator of this foul play by the heel—indeed, you may assume not only my co-operation, to that end, but also that of all my staff. The man must, without question, be brought to retribution." Sergeant Sump made a mental note: Miss Vulpitude had pointed out how often in conventional tributes any mention of women is omitted; it seemed a fair rejoinder to point out that usually only men are thought of as suspects in murder cases. "In the interests of discretion, however, in the public interest if you will, I hope that no unnecessary scandal need arrive. The murderer, by his one heinous act, has already gravely hurt the corporation. Always provided he is caught, it would be untoward, would it not, to add further, and wantonly, to the damage he has made."

"Well," the inspector replied, "we don't actually make a habit of slinging mud in every possible direction. What has to come out, as evidence, will have to come out. But I think you can rely on us to use a certain amount of discretion. There's no question of suppressing evidence, of course. But we aren't out to injure the innocent. Anyway, for all we know yet, this may turn out to be an entirely private crime: the CBC's reputation may not be involved at all."

The president caught the implied nuance: "But you don't expect it to be a private crime, no?"

"We have an open mind," the inspector replied. "Some of us are working on that possibility, elsewhere. Here, it's our task to investigate the professional possibility." He paused. "In that connection, sir, you were saying a moment ago we could count on the co-operation of your staff. We may need access to information that would ordinarily be confidential. I wonder if you could give a memo to Miss Vulpitude authorizing us to poke our noses in where we need to."

"Certainly, certainly." An uncomfortable interview was drawing to an end, and the president was affable. "Was there anything else you gentlemen wished to discuss while the opportunity offers itself?"

Sergeant Sump spoke up. "Just one thing, sir. Do you yourself happen to know anyone who might have wanted to kill Henry Midden?"

The president's affability vanished, like a light switched off.

He flushed. "It is not my habitude, Sergeant, to consort with murderers. For you it may be a professional necessity. For myself, such associations are neither needful nor, I assure you, desired."

"Oh sure." Sergeant Sump wasn't that easily snubbed. "But that wasn't what I asked you. I just wanted to know if you could think of anyone who might want Mr. Midden out of the way."

Obliged to answer, but wishing to put the sergeant in his place, President Laval ignored him and turned to his superior. "To the best of my knowledge, Inspector," he said stiffly, "no officer of this corporation has ever deviated, or would, from his loyalty to our late general manager. And until you show me reason to believe otherwise, I shall continue to presume, with him as with all his colleagues, that in his private life his conduct was that of a gentleman." He rose to go. "I shall now dictate that memorandum. And I trust you will keep me posted."

The door closed behind him.

"Seem to have touched a sore spot, don't I," Sergeant Sump ventured. "Anyone'd think he had something to hide. You don't suppose . . ."

"No, Fred, I don't suppose. But I do admit the possibility. Could be another case of King David and Uriah the Hittite."

"Come off it, Andrew. You know what kind of mick upbringing I had. Lots of mass and confession, and Latin up to here. But we never had the Bible pounded into us like you Protestants. What's with Uriah the Hittite?"

The inspector cast a recollective eye toward the ceiling— funny how childhood habits assert themselves, he thought: God is always Up There. " 'And it came to pass in an eveningtide,' " he began, " 'that David arose from off his bed, and walked upon the roof of the king's house: and from the roof he saw a woman washing herself; and the woman was very beautiful to look upon.' In other words, the Royal Person was a Peeping Tom. And the fact it was another man's wife he got horny over wasn't about to stand in his path: kings, after all, were

81

used to having their own way. So he arranged for the husband Uriah to get killed in a battle, and then he annexed the widow. Mind you, I'm not suggesting any exact parallel. Murder isn't usually needed these days as an entrée to adultery; so I doubt if there's much future in looking for a liaison between Laval and Mrs. Midden. But I do suggest we ought to keep in mind that Midden's death wasn't necessarily contrived from below: it could have been done from above. If so, we probably have to ask ourselves, not what Laval would stand to gain from his death, but what he would stand to lose if Midden went on living."

"Yeah. But that's going to take a bit of digging. One thing's for sure: if there is any dirt, we won't find it in any of the files he's opening up for us."

"Well, we may not have to bother," the inspector said. "For starters, let's find out if he was home in Ottawa last night. Do you want to add his name to the list of people to be checked?"

Sergeant Sump smiled. "I already did."

"Anything else, Fred?"

"Yeah, this stranger off the street (pardon me, this 'foreigner'), I thought he pushed that a little bit too hard. If he's as smart as I think he is, there's something to that." The inspector made as if to interrupt, but the sergeant waved him off. "I mean, it's so unlikely, he may have been pushing it for a reason: to nudge us away from it, towards thinking even more strongly it must be an inside job or a private one. Which would be greatly to his advantage, if he's hired a pro to do the dirty work but had covered his own tracks and got an alibi."

"Fred, have you been reading detective stories again?" The sergeant came as near to blushing as his florid countenance allowed: it was his one vice; he was a like a gourmet with an occasional perverse taste for ketchup. "It won't do, it won't do. The reasoning's all very sound, but you overlook the primary facts of the killing: this wasn't a pro job, and you know it. A bomb in his car, yes. Or a long-distance shot with a telescopic lens. Or sometimes, with the clever ones, a kidnapping, then contact the client for a higher fee before polishing him off. But this, no. Your pro doesn't pick a scene like this in the first place: subject to unpredictable interruption by a night watchman; and time-consuming, because (as a 'total foreigner') he'd have to lull the victim's suspicions first if he was going to choose so crude and unreliable a method as a blow on the head without leaving any signs of a struggle, for God's sake." The inspector paused for a well-earned breath. "Agreed?"

"Okay, it wasn't a pro job: it was someone he knew. But that doesn't rule out conspiracy: Laval and a sidekick."

"You do like to make life complicated, don't you, Fred? Anyone would think you didn't trust the president."

"No more do you and you know it. He's too smooth. And I don't like the way he talks. It doesn't ring true."

"Yes, but you have to make allowances for the fact that he's speaking a second language. You must have noticed how different people sometimes seem in a second language from the way they are in their mother tongue." The inspector was not an exponent of *different than*. "It's like wearing clothes that don't fit. You can't act naturally."

"Sometimes," the sergeant replied. "But not always. Some people manage to be completely themselves in a second language, even if they don't speak it well: people who have a good secure sense of who they are. On the other hand, I've found that people who sound phony in a second language usually sound pretty phony in their mother tongue too: role-players— in a sense con men, even if they don't earn their living at it. You can usually tell by looking at their eyes when they smile."

"Well, that's your department." The inspector had a solid trust in his colleague's feeling for people. "But I must admit he did sound rather like a politician. Not that that necessarily means anything: men with that bent never get off their platform. Who's next?"

As if on cue, Miss Vulpitude knocked at the door and came in. "Mr. Lew Stukely is here," she announced.

83

SIX

Tuesday, 2:30–3:00

PROGRAM SCHEDULE #5: *Tuesday 2:30–3:00*

AM SERVICE

2:30 "Today," a magazine for afternoon listeners with co-hosts Judith Fogg and Paul Zonk. Featured on the first part of today's edition: the new C&W recording by Butterscotch; a conversation with Marvin Fitch, secretary of the Cosmic-Frisbee Association in Hangnail, Alberta; and Paul has the fifty-third in his three-year course of tuba lessons (this week he tackles E flat).

FM SERVICE

2:30 "Collage" continues. The second part of this afternoon's program will include "Introduction, Rubric, and Prayer" by Arnoldo Belmont; "Seven Sacred Limericks" by Dean Ullyot; and "O admirable et bone Gautama," an ecumenical motet by Calvin Moses.

LEW STUKELY WAS, to all outward appearances, the archetypical ordinary man. Of medium height and build, he dressed in the vogue of the day and spoke, colorlessly, in whatever patois was currently passing for English. Yet there was, to any astute observer, a touch of deliberation in all this averageness, as though it were cultivated and assumed rather than genuinely his own. Some men are born average, Sergeant Sump reflected, priding themselves on a kind of anonymity; some achieve that state; and some have averageness thrust upon them, leaving no record of their lives except as statistics in a sociological report. The interesting ones, usually, were the ones who achieved mediocrity as a goal. Their motive, as a rule, was either fear or gain: the fearful would not risk rejection by their peers; the greedy saw in conformity the highway to success—and this latter type was especially common among politicians and swindlers.

Sergeant Sump checked himself. He must not let himself be influenced by Henry Midden's memo: Lew Stukely might or might not have been guilty, once, of taking kickbacks; but nothing had been proved. Until proof appeared, it seemed fairer to take him at face value: as the average broadcaster serving the average listener of average tastes.

Yet, somehow, it wouldn't wash. The answer to his very first question had struck a false note. Faintly—but unmistakably. "I guess Henry Midden was your boss," he had begun. "What sort of man was he?"

And Stukely had replied: "Well, of course, he was pretty close to retiring age. But he really stayed in touch, you know: with the public. As long as the ratings stayed up there, he was happy. Not too popular with some of our arty types, maybe. But he knew what the public liked, and that's what counts. We got along pretty good."[1]

This was not so much a portrait of a man as a summation of a work pattern. And Sergeant Sump discerned a good deal more in it than Stukely had perhaps meant him to. In the first place, here was another person harping on the theme of Midden's approaching retirement, and doing so, it seemed, almost by reflex. There comes a time when any potentate's days are clearly numbered; but people don't usually start counting them quite that pointedly, unless he's either irreplaceable (like Pope John) or heartily detested (like Franco). Then, too, there was something almost gratuitous and overeager about his attempt, at this early stage, to divert suspicion from himself: he and Midden may have gotten along pretty well, and Midden may have been disliked by the 'arty types' (whoever they might be); but bringing the matter up so early, and unprompted, tended

---

[1] Critics, during this period, were not convinced that the CBC was right in its quest for easy popularity. They contended that its proper task was the pursuit of excellence; and excellence could not be achieved by catering to the lowest common denominator of public taste, for the sake of high ratings. On television this program policy took the form of importing the shallowest American productions, or imitating them. On radio two tactics were used: on the one hand, all work of substance was banished to the ghetto of FM; on the other hand, AM concentrated on soap operas, Muzak, and gossip. The paradoxical result was that the CBC almost entirely lost the base of popular support it needed: its only remaining defenders seemed to be those Canadians who lived within reach of FM radio, plus a few more who wished they did.

to suggest that relations between the two men might, in reality, have been less than cordial. Finally, there was the fact that Stukely's answer had not, in any direct way, addressed itself to the question. Sergeant Sump had often noticed how people, when asked something specific, will take refuge in a reply which has a loose connection with the subject but which essentially deals with something else; this kind of response frequently stemmed from anxiety or guilt, but sometimes it only denoted preoccupation with a pet topic or even mere inattention. In this case, there was no means of knowing, yet.

"Did you kill him?" The best way to deal with evasiveness, Sergeant Sump reckoned, was to stop it in its tracks. And a blunt, rude question like this might serve the extra purpose of flustering the witness: in a successful interrogation the interrogator always keep control of the conversation, its pace, its tone, and its content.

Stukely flushed. "That's a pretty rotten thing to suggest, Sergeant," he said. "I came here to try and be helpful. But if you want to just sit there and make groundless accusations . . ." He sputtered into an indignant silence.

"Actually, I didn't accuse you of anything," Sergeant Sump retorted. "But it might help if you answered the question."

"Did I kill him?" It was an old technique: repeat the question and gain time to think. The reply, when it came, was poised and cold. "No, I didn't. And I doubt very much if you'll find the culprit by just going around asking *that*."

"Oh, I don't know," Sergeant Sump responded. "You'd be surprised how many culprits give themselves away unconsciously when you ask them that." He paused a moment to let the significance of this sink in. It was a gross exaggeration, as he himself would have been the first to admit; but that was something a suspect wouldn't know. Then he went on: "Anyhow, if you didn't, can you think of anyone who might have wanted to?"

This was the question Sergeant Sump had really been leading up to: first unsettle the witness with a near-accusation, then keep him uneasy with an innuendo, and finally let him off the hook with a chance to point the finger elsewhere; how he used the opportunity might tell a lot. Stukely seized it.

"Not anyone in particular," he said. "But there is, generally speaking, a line of enquiry you might find worth pursuing." He looked down primly at his decorously trousered knees. "How shall I put this? Well, let's just say, Mr. Midden was quite the ladies' man. I mean, it went a bit further than maybe having a girl friend on the side, or having a casual weekend fling when the family was up at the cottage. Nobody's perfect, but Henry made a career of it. You name it, he chased it. Just so long as it wore a skirt, came in somewheres between fifteen and fifty, and wasn't outrageously repulsive, he wanted in. And from all I hear, he scored pretty good, too. Never could make out what he'd got that the rest of us haven't. But then, I guess if we all knew the answer to that, we'd have a hard time keeping the old home fire burning, wouldn't we?"

He delivered himself of this sententious euphemism with all the cheery self-righteousness of a married man who was only kept from infidelities by the fear of being caught.

"Mind you," he continued, "I've no idea where he'd been sleeping around recently, or who with. And if I did know, I'm not sure I'd care to tell you. In fact, I'm only telling you this much because I figure you'd be bound to dig it out anyway. A man can't screw around like Henry did without it being pretty well known. And frankly, I'm surprised it didn't catch up with him earlier. Not like this, I mean"—Stukely made a vague gesture deprecating violent death as too steep a price to pay for fornication—"but something was bound to happen eventually. You can't lay every piece in a fifty-mile radius without upsetting a few people in the course of it."

For a moment Sergeant Sump wondered if this was going to be the first recorded case of a murder committed out of envy. But then he considered what he'd heard, and realised his tactics had paid off. The answer to his question had revealed two things which the speaker had not intended to convey: first, that he had indeed borne some degree of malice towards the deceased; and second, that he wished to steer enquiries towards a private motive, away from professional ones.

He resumed his questioning. "When did you last see Mr. Midden yourself?"

"Well, he and I were pretty much running into each other all day every day, you know. Our jobs interlocked. Yesterday wasn't any different." For a moment Stukely hesitated, obviously not wanting to implicate himself with the victim beyond the sacred hour of five o'clock, and especially not up to a late-evening hour that might be close to the time of the killing. But then he evidently realised there had been too many people at the evening meeting for him to have any hope of concealing his attendance. "At least, no different during the day: a lot of casual contacts on and off. But then, afterwards, we both worked late. Us and a few others. Had a meeting right here in this office. Went on most of the evening. So I guess I last saw Henry about ten forty-five: I just got home in time for the eleven o'clock news."

"You live close by then?" It was Inspector Coggin's first interjection.

"Yes, just a couple of blocks. Means I don't have to bother with the car—thank God."

"And who else was at the meeting?" The inspector was not about to be drawn off into another discussion of traffic problems.

"Let's see. There was Joyce Parchment, of course: she's my opposite number in FM. And Bud Benedict: he's head of Outside Broadcasts. And Arnold Gloss, our P.R. man. Oh yes, and Norm Casement: he's in charge of our technical side."

"Did you all stay to the end?" This kind of questioning was the inspector's territory: dealt with factual detail, the sergeant with intangibles. "Or did some of you manage to get away earlier?"

"No, we were all involved right through. Mind you, we didn't leave as a group. Most of us drive down, so the others would head for the parking lot while I wouldn't. And anyway, Henry was going to stay on and get a few other things dealt with—so was Arnold. So I guess it was just Joyce and Bud headed for the parking lot, come to think of it. Norm made a big thing about needing to go to the can."

"And this was about ten forty-five, you figure."

"That's right, yes."

"Did you actually see Mrs. Parchment or Mr. Benedict drive off?"

"As a matter of fact I did. My way home takes me up past the parking lot, and I hadn't gone more than half a block when she came wheeling out—waved good night as she drove by. And Bud was right behind her in his car."

Sergeant Sump looked up. "What sort of a meeting was it, Mr. Stukely?" he asked. "Just an ordinary sort of business meeting? Or would you say there was anything about it which struck you as different from what you'd usually expect?"

"No, it was normal enough. What way different d'you mean?"

"Oh, just were there any big arguments or anything? Any signs of personality conflicts?"

"Nothing out of the way. We always argue, of course. But not so as you'd call it getting personal with each other. Besides, we didn't have anything to get personal about: it was just practicalities mainly—like the old punch line in the limerick, 'who does which and with what and to whom.' No big deal."

"I see." Sergeant Sump smiled,[2] but pressed on. "What kind of practicalities?"

"Oh, all the changes we're going to have to make in our program schedule in the fall: for the Canada Youth Festival. Like deciding which events would make good programs; and which ones belonged on AM or FM; and what programs to pre-empt to make room for them; and did those programs have enough

[2] Later, at leisure, Inspector Coggin asked him to complete the stanza alluded to. It ran: "A lesbian girl in Khartoum / Took a pansy boy up to her room;/As she turned out the light,/She said to him, 'Right,/Who does which and with what and to whom?' "

93

budget to pay for their replacements; and did we have the gear and the personnel for all the coverage; and how much mileage could we get out of the publicity. That sort of thing."

"Get it all straightened away?"

"Yeah, most of it anyways." Stukely chuckled reminiscently. "Old Norm had a great time—that's Norm Casement, our operations man. He has a real down on some of our producers: you know, the long-hair kind that think all that highbrow crap's the only stuff that matters; we've got a couple of real lulus here in Toronto." Inspector Coggin remembered having read press rumours, from time to time, about internecine war at the CBC, and poor morale in the ranks: he began, now, to give these some credence. "So anyways," Stukely resumed, "Norm figured a way to settle their hash for a while: came up with two spare crews and equipment so we can send them out on assignment. One of them spends most of his time frigging around with electronic chamber music—sounds like a banshee gone berserk in a hardware store—and we're packing him off to Hernia Falls: they're putting on a Nostalgia Week there, and they've asked for someone to come down and mount a re-creation of the Saturday night dance-remotes we used to do thirty years ago; that'll fix *him*. And the other one, she's an artsy-fartsy drama producer—you know the kind: read the telephone directory backwards through an echo chamber and you've got Significance—well, sir, she's just going to have to climb down off her high horse for a while and come to grips with reality: we're lending her to Kate Aitken Memorial College in Verruca, Saskatchewan. They have a radio and television department there, and she's going to have to give a course on 'The Craft of Soap Opera,' ending up with a student production of a tear-jerker called *Generation Gap*. All told, things should be nice and quiet around here for a while, with those two gone."

Sergeant Sump concluded he should not read any special meaning into Stukely's earlier swipe at people in Production: it was clearly just part of a general hostility to that area, and not a specific insinuation that some unbearably intellectual producer might actually have smashed Henry Midden's skull.

"I suppose we can corroborate your getting home at eleven, eh?" Inspector Coggin was back to his basic spadework. "Someone there who can confirm it?"

"Oh sure," laconically. "My wife was in."

"And once you were home, you stayed in?"

The inspector frequently told recruits they must never be ashamed to ask obvious questions: nothing can be assumed. This time his principle paid off. Stukely paused and flushed, obviously gunned his brain for a choice of answer, and then said, "Well, actually, no I didn't. Couple of floors up in our apartment block a bunch of guys I know were having a friendly poker game, so I dropped in for a few hands—supposed to be there earlier, but the meeting got in the way."

"Stay long?"

"No, only a few hands: the cards weren't going right." He anticipated the next question. "I guess I was out of there by half-past twelve."

"And you went straight back to your own apartment?"

"Yeah." He grinned ruefully. "Mind you, I can't prove it. My wife was asleep, and I didn't meet anyone on the way."

"Well, I don't think we need concern ourselves overmuch with that, Mr. Stukely." Since there was no way of pursuing that point at the moment, the inspector could afford to seem magnanimous. "Perhaps you'd just tell us which apartment the poker game was in, and who was there; then we'll at least have you accounted for till the time you left."

Stukely became visibly uncomfortable again. With obvious reluctance he gave them the address and named four fellow card players. His reluctance was understandable: all of them were well-known gamblers and three of them had criminal records. These three, as crooks, were extremely small-time; and Sergeant Sump sensed that some of Stukely's embarrassment stemmed from snobbery: if you have to be caught consorting with undesirables, at least try and make it a cut above the riffraff. He also had a hunch that the list was incomplete: "That's all who were there, eh?" he asked. "Nobody else joined you."

A tiny pause, and a just perceptible effort at nonchalance, confirmed his hunch.

"No. No one."

Inspector Coggin made a note to check this point out. While he was contemplating its possible implications (which probably had nothing to do with the case at hand, but might have a great deal to do with the shadiness of Stukely's character), Sergeant Sump seized upon this moment of discomfiture to spring a seemingly unrelated question.

"Oh, by the way, Mr. Stukely, does the name Atisbar mean anything to you? Dr. Atisbar?"

Time and again in their work they had seen it happen, and it happened now: the scarcely discernible change of gears, as in a well-oiled automatic transmission, then the smooth functioning of an open and natural demeanour: everything exactly in place: the tone of voice, the flow of words halfway between fluent and inarticulate, the look of the eyes neither bold nor evasive, a few apparently unself-conscious gestures. As an imitation of innocent co-operative response, it was perfect. Its only, but fatal, flaw was its perfection. No one, outside the acting profession, is that efficient at conveying the effect of a candour that wholly lacks artifice—no one, that is, except for highly skilled criminals or their near-counterparts, topflight salesmen. It takes a kind of virtuoso dishonesty to portray, so exactly, the honest man.

"Atisbar? No, I don't think so. Oh, but wait a minute. Wasn't he the fellow they imported from some think tank in the States? MIT or some place like that? Yes, I remember. Little guy with horn-rimmed glasses. Came here to check out our management techniques and tell us everything we were doing wrong. That who you mean?"

"Yes." Sergeant Sump was impressed: it was an adroit performance. "Who did he report to?"

"Well, I imagine to Henry Midden. Can't say for sure, though. So far as I know, the whole thing kind of fizzled out. At least, there were never any results circulated that I saw."

Sergeant Sump decided to improvise. "Oh, I rather had the impression it might be a sort of time bomb. According to what I've heard, Dr. Atisbar was extremely critical of things around here, and management was thinking of making quite a few hard-nosed changes."

This gambit put Stukely in an awkward position, since he couldn't be sure how much the police knew. His only safe response was to admit the possibility that a corporate house cleaning was in prospect, but to dissociate himself from it. "Well," he said carefully, "I guess you can't investigate a place this big without finding a few things wrong here and there. But I don't know that management aimed to stage any kind of large-scale witch hunt."

"Oh, probably not." Sergeant Sump was at his most cordially agreeable—a sure sign to Inspector Coggin of the fang behind the smile. "I mean, you're obviously right that there wouldn't be a concerted campaign of firings and resignations: that sort of thing does far too much damage to a corporation's image. But in a scattered way, there must have been several individuals who felt threatened. I just thought I'd ask you about it because I figured you'd be in a position to know."

"You mean, whose head was going to roll?"

"Yes, I guess so." Sergeant Sump leant forward earnestly. "Let me put it this way. I'm not suggesting the CBC was cram full of incompetents. But any corporation this size is bound to have some dead wood in it: people who've been promoted beyond their ability, or grown tired or lazy or out of date; perhaps even one or two real bad apples, cases of actual corruption."

"Oh sure, we're no different than anyone else as far as that— I dare say even the Police Department isn't completely immune. But it's not that easy to deal with. What we usually do is try and ease these guys into early retirement. Or, if they're not old enough, we recognise so their posts become redundant and then we can move them into some other job they can handle. There's usually a way round most cases without having to put a guy out on the street."

Stukely produced this humanitarian flourish with aplomb and satisfaction. However, it had the air of something learnt from a manual rather than something felt. And Sergeant Sump reflected that here was a case of having your cake and eating it: if Stukely fostered a tradition of suffering fools gladly, or crooks, he could gain a reputation for kindliness while at the same time warding off any threat to his own tenure; any threat, that is, that might stem from his being either a fool or a crook himself. The time had now come to confront that point.

"All right," he said, "that's fine for the charity cases. But how about the ones that are a bit more serious? I presume you can't stick to the kid gloves when you're faced with that sort of thing."

"What sort of thing?" Stukely hedged.

Sergeant Sump was quite willing to be explicit. "Any serious breach of ethics. Not necessarily illegal. In fact, corruption usually manages to stay inside the law. But most decent people know it when they see it." He expanded. "Even in high places it's often something extraordinarily shabby. You'd be amazed what big stakes are risked for a petty gain or a sleazy favour. And that's what it boils down to—gain or favour: when someone goes wrong like that, as a rule it's for one of two reasons: either greed or lust." These old-fashioned, blunt monosyllables had an odd ring to them in a room whose customary fare was euphemism and circumlocution.

Stukely parried adroitly, and with good humour. "I know what you mean. They've had a helluva big scandal over that sort of thing twice in recent years at the BBC. One was the disc-jockey business: disc-jockeys pushing certain records on the air and being given free women in return. The other time, which didn't get so much publicity, was actually a lot more serious and a lot more widespread: the place was jammed with queers—administrators, producers, you name it—and there was all kinds of nepotism involved; not just in pay raises and so on, but every time there was a vacancy another queer would get the job. That was a real mess, that one."

Sergeant Sump steered the conversation back from England to Canada. "Anything of that sort go on here?"

"Not so as it counts for anything. Mind you, I can't answer for television: there are a few places over there where I wouldn't want to bend over and tie my shoelaces. But here in radio it's pretty straight. At least, as far as the men are concerned. We do have a bit of a problem in the Religious Department: it's headed up by an ex-nun who's gay, and nobody much seems to work there except other dykes. But that's a tough area to point your finger at: anything you might try to do would backfire like as not; they're too strong, in terms of public support—I mean, badmouthing them would be next door to painting 'Fuck Jesus' on a church wall, and you know where that'd get you."

It crossed Inspector Coggin's mind that the question had not arisen, had evidently not seemed worth mentioning, of whether or not the Religious Department's work, as contrasted with its after-hours proclivities, was any good. He wondered at what level of seniority such considerations ceased to matter. Meanwhile Sergeant Sump, passing up the unexplored territory of heterosexual graft, had moved to the attack.

"Yes," he replied, "I can see that. You mean, even if they did feel threatened, they wouldn't have to hit anyone over the head with a blunt instrument; they could simply fall back on the support of their constituency. Pity! It'd made a great headline in *Midnight*: 'Gay Nun Brains Boss—Broadcaster Found in Pool of Blood—Lesbian Vice-Ring Accused of Human Sacrifice.' Ah well, as you say, it's not very likely. That leaves us with money. Now, there's a good, strong motive. Anyone around here suspected of taking kickbacks?"

Murder by Microphone

The question had all the casual offhand quality of a remark about the weather. But Inspector Coggin, although he was much less sensitive to the nuances of human emotion than he was alert to subtle relationships of fact, was acutely aware of the tension between the two men—despite the apparent candour, the air of courtesy.

"No, definitely not." Stukely's reply was altogether too prompt and emphatic. And he compounded his blunder by immediately talking about what would come first to the mind of an embezzler contemplating a job. "Actually, it'd be very hard to pull off anything like that. Our system of contracting and paying artists has to be right out in the open, for tax reasons. So everything would have to be on a cash basis, and word of mouth. And quite frankly, I can't imagine anyone being that stupid: if somebody wanted to turn you in, all he need do would be to pay you off with marked bills. No, the only way I can see anyone risking it, would be if he had some kind of hold over the victims which would keep their mouths shut. Of course, there's always artistic vanity as a sort of protection: most performers would rather drop dead than admit they got work through kickbacks and not because of their talent. But having some other kind of hold over them, too, would be useful extra insurance."

As he spoke, Stukely had quickly recovered his poise and, with it, a light conversational tone. But the effort of doing so had forced him to concentrate on presentation rather than content. How he said what he said was innocent-sounding enough. What he said, though, betrayed a mind used to thinking along such lines.

This was not lost on Sergeant Sump. "You're probably right," he said. "But that doesn't mean no such person exists. The world's full of crooks. As you yourself said, if the Police Department isn't immune from them, why should the CBC be? And I can imagine, in such a case, if the guilty party felt he was going to be exposed, he might well resort to murder, to protect himself."

The only possible response to this was silence.

"So," Sergeant Sump concluded, "if you should run across any indication of something like that having gone wrong—or anything else that might be relevant—we'd appreciate your letting us know." He stood up. "But for the time being I think that about wraps things up. Unless the inspector has anything he wants to add."

"No, not right now. That'll be all for the moment, Mr. Stukely. And thanks very much for your help. We'll keep in touch, eh?"

After the door had closed, Inspector Coggin made a phone call and assigned four men to contact Stukely's fellow poker players of the previous night. All of them were readily found, and the results of the enquiry were in before the afternoon was over. Independently all four corroborated Stukely's statement that he had been there from shortly after eleven until approximately half-past twelve. Questioned further, they vindicated Sergeant Sump's hunch: a sixth man had indeed been there, whose presence Stukely had denied. All four witnesses agreed that this man had arrived during the last hand of cards before Stukely left, that his arrival had seemed to have some connection with Stukely's departure, and that the two of them had left together. This sixth man was known to all of them, and they named him.

His name was also known to Inspector Coggin and to Sergeant Sump. He was an enforcer.

SEVEN

Tuesday, 3:00–3:30

PROGRAM SCHEDULE ♯6: *Tuesday 3:00–3:30*

3:00 News

3:04 "Today" continues. On the second part of today's edition: Purple Ketchup, recorded at the pre-teen love-in
on Rump Island, Nfld; "Your Destiny," a phone-in, with
Darius Lumen, assistant astrologer to the federal cabinet; and "Barf," a mini-documentary about confron-
tation politics in the high schools, taped during the cafeteria sick-in at Fleming Collegiate in Thorax, Manitoba.

3:00 "Collage" continues. The third part of this afternoon's
program will include the Concerto ♯183 in F for con-
trabassoon and strings by Georg Philipp Lohnschreiber;
Metaphysickal Ode by Titus Vetch of Todmorden; and
Giovanni Giovedi's *Wedding Cantata* for the nuptials
of Felix, Archduke of Aufrichtung und Steifheit, and
Princess Constanze von Eintritt-Oftmals.

With Norm Casement, Sergeant Sump came directly to the point. Bluntly. It was the only available tactic. In the ring, a boxer can outpoint the sluggers and win: he can expose their lack of skill and lower their ranking; but he will not find out where they hurt. In a police interrogation, finding out where they hurt is all-important: it matters far more than scoring conversational points. So, faced with a slugger, it behooved Sergeant Sump to be a harder, ruggeder, slugger; and to get his blow in first. Besides, there was always the possibility that Casement's rhinocerine approach might prove to be a façade: half the world's bullies are chicken on the inside, and ashamed of it; a few solid hooks and jabs would show if the brawn and belligerence were real or hollow.

"Mr. Casement," he began, "I have to tell you that Henry Midden's death was undoubtedly murder. We don't know yet who did it. But whoever did it, planned it. That means we're looking for someone who had a grudge against him or was in conflict with him. Either professionally or in his private life. Or both. And in his professional life, that takes in quite a lot of people. You're one of them. Needless to say, I hope it turns out you're innocent. But it's only fair to let you know where we stand. There are some questions we'd like to ask you, and any help you can give us will be much appreciated. However, you don't have to answer them if you don't want to."

Inspector Coggin immediately followed this up by reciting his legal rights to the suspect, and making sure they were understood. Throughout, Casement remained entirely impassive. His heavy, mottled face gave nothing away; the thick body and legs, quiet and relaxed; the arms and hands, composed and still. He might as easily have been listening to a livestock report. And it was impossible to say whether this was self-control or indifference. "Those are your rights," the inspector finished. "We're obliged to tell you them. But of course what we really need is your assistance."

This conclusion seemed to call for some kind of response, which made it hard for Sergeant Sump to pitch in at once with his questioning. Casement clearly discerned this, and let them dangle a while in a silence of their own making. Then he looked stolidly from one to the other, creased his face into a humourless smile, and said, "Okay, now you're through with the bullshit, what do you want to know?"

Sergeant Sump sailed right in. "I'd like you to describe your movements yesterday evening, after the end of the meeting. When did you leave?"

"Same time as everyone else. Around ten forty-five, I guess."

"Everyone?"

"Well, no, not exactly," Casement conceded. "I mean, that's when the meeting broke up. Lew Stukely went home then, as far as I know, and so did Joyce Parchment and Bud Benedict. Arnold Gloss stayed on, to go over a couple of things with Henry. And that's the last I saw of him."

"After you'd gone to the can, did you go straight home?" Sergeant Sump was a firm believer in the well-timed leading question, blatantly used.

"Oh, you know about that, do you?" Casement seemed not in the least ruffled. "No, I didn't. Fact is, I didn't even need to go to the can. I just said I had to so the others would leave without me. I figured maybe Arnold wouldn't take too long with Henry, and there was something I wanted to see Henry about myself."

"But it didn't work out, eh?"

"No, I got back from the can and they were still in here together, with the door closed. I'd have come in perhaps, except I could hear them, even out there in Vulpitude's office, and they were having a helluva fight. Verbal, of course: you wouldn't find Arnold Gloss getting physical—not even with a sonofabitch like Henry." This was said with unabashed dislike of the deceased, and with evident contempt for a man who wouldn't back his words up with his fists.

"What were they fighting about? Could you hear?" Sergeant Sump reckoned he wasn't interrogating the kind of man who'd be fussy about a bit of eavesdropping, or even about admitting to it.

"Near as I could tell, about his wife."

"Whose wife?"

"Arnold's." Casement grinned again, joylessly. "Henry'd been into her a couple of times and Arnold was pretty upset. Mind you, I couldn't make out everything they were saying— only when they raised their voices—but that was the general drift."

"So then what happened?"

"Well, there didn't seem to be much point in sticking around waiting for Henry, with something like that going on. God knows how long it might have lasted. So I just sat down at Vulpitude's desk and phoned home to say I was on my way."

"And then you left?"

"No. I'd just got through calling when they got through scrapping. I don't know, maybe they heard me using the phone and were embarrassed into quitting, or maybe they were about through anyway. Anyway, I'd no sooner hung up than Arnold walked out of here, looking like he'd been through a wringer; and I'm damn sure he wasn't pleased to see me."

Inspector Coggin interjected one of his precise questions of detail: "From where you were sitting, could you see through into this office?"

"Not to any extent. Besides, Arnold shut the door behind him as he came out." Again the hostile smile. "But if you mean, did I see Henry stretched out on the rug with his brains bashed in, no I didn't. As I told you, I never saw Henry again. And anyway, I happen to know he was alive when we left."

"How so?"

"Because just as I was getting up from Vulpitude's phone, one of Henry's locals lit up with an outgoing call; so he must have been alive and well in order to place it."

Inspector Coggin ignored the possibility that a mortally wounded man is sometimes known to try and phone for help. "You just said, 'we left,'" he countered. "You left together?"

"Yes. And if you're thinking Arnold maybe came back later and knocked him off, I can tell you he didn't. Because Arnold's car was on the fritz yesterday morning and he'd left it home. So I gave him a lift in my car. Which means not only can I corroborate his leaving, but he can corroborate my leaving. Which lets us both out, I guess." This time the smile had noticeable relish to it.

"Well, yes, perhaps it does, up to a point," Sergeant Sump agreed. "Always provided you can both account for your whereabouts later. For instance, where does Mr. Gloss live? When did you get there? Did you just drop him off, or did you go in with him? How long did it take you to go home from there, and where do you live? And when you got home, did you stay there and can you prove it?" These questions were delivered with rapidity and force: a good slugger can take his man out with one punch; but a good, canny slugger knows how and when to be a combination puncher too.

Casement rode with the lot. "How's about giving me that

again, one at a time?" he requested. And given a repeat, he described how he drove Arnold Gloss to his home in Don Mills, which took twenty-five minutes, and dropped him off, and drove on for a further twenty minutes in the same general direction to his own home in Scarborough, and went to bed, and his wife would confirm that.

Inspector Coggin began to ponder which of his available men might be the best one to interview Mrs. Casement: to find out, tactfully, what kind of relationship she enjoyed with her husband, and especially to find out if there were any possibility he could have slipped her a strong sleeping pill and then gone out again unbeknownst to her.

Meanwhile, Sergeant Sump was asking one of his superficially casual questions. "By the way, what was it you wanted to see Mr. Midden about yourself? It must have been pretty private, the way you went about it."

"It was." There was no trace of a smile now. "What I had to say to that bastard was strictly between he and I." Inspector Coggin winced. Casement continued. "I'd have as soon wrung his neck as not, but that wasn't anybody else's business but ours. And yours now too, I guess." He looked at them both bleakly. "You may as well have it from me, since I suppose you'd find out anyway. I'm glad he's dead, and I'm sorry it wasn't me did it."

Sergeant Sump also knew when to be silent. Casement was just as aggressive now in his demeanour; but his tone had come honest; and back of what he was saying, a hurt lurked, willing at last to admit its own existence.

"Ever heard of a program called 'String Along'?" he asked. "Light classics and old favourites for strings? Maybe you haven't. But it's good even if I do say so myself. My daughter does it. And if you think that's nepotism, a girl getting a program whose father's in the business, I can assure you I have nothing whatever to do with the program side of things around here: I'm in Operations. But I tell you who does, though—did, rather. Henry Midden did. And do you know what she had to do to get that program? She had to let him screw her. I didn't find out at the time—that was three months ago—and it's just as well for Henry that I didn't. Chances are I never would have found out if she hadn't got pregnant and turned to me for help for an abortion because her husband was away on a six-month assignment, so he obviously wasn't the father and would have known he wasn't. She made me promise not to do anything about it, so far as Henry was concerned: she felt too ashamed. But I didn't figure that promise applied to the next stage in the whole rotten business. Having put her on the air, Henry seemed to think he had her where he wanted her. So what does he do but tell her she'd better keep on coming across; if not, he'll cancel the program. That's when I decided Henry had to be stopped."

There was a heavy silence. Inspector Coggin reflected, dismally, on justice: on how improbable it was that anyone, knowing the circumstances, would for a moment allow that Casement's daughter's program might, in fact, be good, that she might have deserved her job. And Sergeant Sump reflected ruefully on mercy: what had promised to be a slugfest had turned out, through no skill or strength of his own, to be a walkover; and, in the circumstances, his nature leaned to mercy, towards this crestfallen opponent—and his training forbade it. There's no more efficient con job, experience told him, than one which is based on the truth; to sympathise with such a man, in such a predicament, cannot expunge him from the list of suspects. "How?" he asked finally. "How did you propose to stop him?"

"Oh, I didn't look for him to give me any trouble." A tinge of his former self-assertion came back into Casement's voice. "Even at his age, Henry could still have got fired, I guess, if I'd blown the whistle on him. At that stage it wouldn't have affected him financially. But it'd have been more than his ego could stand. All I'd have to do would be tell him to keep his hands off Barbie and leave her program on; or else. He'd have known what I meant."

"But you didn't?"

"Didn't what?"

"Didn't go through with it last night?"

"No." Casement paused. "I'm not exactly sure why. Something to do with that fight he and Arnold had—didn't seem right to go ahead, somehow. Not that I gave a shit about Henry; if it was rough on him, tough titty. I guess, in a way, it was just a stubborn streak, or something. If I was going to blitz Henry, that was up to me; I didn't need someone like Arnold softening him up for me first." He paused again. "Tell you the truth, by the time I got home I regretted it: might just as well have got it over and done with."

"You sure you didn't come back down, then, and get it over and done with?"

"No, I didn't. Not with words. And not with the traditional blunt instrument either."

"Well, it might have come to that if you had come back, you know," Sergeant Sump rejoined. "It's all very well to say he would have backed down if you'd threatened to blow the whistle on him. But what if he'd stood his ground? He might just as easily have told you to go fly a kite. After all, if he cancelled your daughter's program right then and there, anything you said or anything she said would simply look like sour grapes. You wouldn't have had a leg to stand on. What would you have done then?"

"Bashed his brains in, I guess." Casement sighed. "Except I didn't. Somebody else did." His wolfish grin reappeared. "Whoever it was had a helluva good idea."

On that abrasive note, the interview concluded. After the door shut, Sergeant Sump turned to the inspector. "You know something, Andrew?" he said. "I believe him. I don't much like him, and he doesn't strike me as being particularly scrupulous, but I think he was telling the truth."

"Me too," the inspector said. "Most of the time."

"But not all of the time?"

"Well, I wonder. It largely depends on just how clever he is

112

—and that, as yet, we don't know. You see, there are two possibilities. Either he's innocent or he's guilty. If he's innocent, he might make a clean breast of everything and trust us to believe him; but he'd be much more likely to hide his hatred for Midden, since presumably only his daughter knew about it and he could figure we wouldn't find out. Then, too, he'd be just as likely to hide it if, in fact, he's guilty, figuring we wouldn't find out in that case either. But if he's guilty *and* really smart, he'd cough it all up right away, for two good reasons: in the first place it'd look bad for him if we found out about it later and he hadn't told us, and in the second place telling us right away would seem so ingenuous it would look like the act of an innocent man."

Sergeant Sump digested this. "Logically, you're right," he said. "But my own gut feeling is, he was telling the truth all the way."

"Possibly so, possibly so." The inspector had had many good reasons, over the years, to trust his colleague's intuitions. "But consider this, Fred: there's one little thing you may have overlooked. Thus far, the only person who knows roughly *how* Midden died is Miss Vulpitude. And we've asked her to keep mum. So how come when Casement mentioned his demise, he spoke of his brains being bashed in?"

Sergeant Sump shrugged, and said, "Oh, I don't figure that was anything more than just his way of talking—he's obviously a very physical man. Four or five generations ago someone in his position would have said he'd horsewhip the man, but that wouldn't necessarily mean he'd literally take him out to the stable and go over him with a horsewhip. For that matter, outraged fathers or husbands aren't usually lethal: beating a guy up is as far as they usually go—leave him to walk around in public with the humiliation. At least, that's true in spur-of-the-moment situations: a few get carried away and actually kill; but most don't. And as for the situations which aren't on the spur of the moment—and that's what we're talking about— most men cool out when they've given it second thoughts. And those that don't"—he cast his mind back a few years to a famous case in Hollywood—"they don't put a gun to the guy's head: they aim it at his crotch."

The inspector cast his mind back even further, to twelfth-century Paris, and Abelard unmanned for Heloïse. His colleague was right.

"However," Sergeant Sump resumed, "if you thought the point was important, about 'bashing his brains in,' why didn't you take him up on it yourself?"

Inspector Coggin grinned ruefully. "I should have done," he admitted. "But I'm afraid my mind was wandering just at that moment. I must be getting old. There were you, pinning him down about his daughter's program of string music, and instead of paying proper attention I started remembering a marvellous modern string work the CBC broadcast years ago by Karl Amadeus Hartmann and thinking what a far cry that is from their present diet of marshmallows. Goes to show you: thirty years in the business and I can still get sidetracked."

"Well, I wouldn't let it bother you. Personally, I don't think the point was of any consequence at all."

Besides, Sergeant Sump reflected to himself, we all have our lapses. He would not soon forget the day, in the Case of the Muted Strumpet, when he had let a perfectly obvious physical clue escape his eye because he had been so engrossed in conversation with the chief suspect, a Chinese miner who had learnt all his English from Scottish emigrés and sounded as though he'd just stepped off the boat from Glasgow. The shoe, then, had been on the other foot.

EIGHT

Tuesday, 3:30–4:00

PROGRAM SCHEDULE ⚇7: *Tuesday* 3:30–4:00

3:30 "Today" continues. On the third part of today's edition: "Blind Date," a weekly chance for lonely listeners to tape their own personal messages and maybe meet the man or woman of their dreams; "Four Pieces of Sticky Fudge," from the latest album by This Way Up; and "Dear Judith," an advice column for listeners with problems—this week's problems have to do with clerical celibacy, and Judith's consultant is Dr. Willi von Jungfleisch, Professor of Applied Erotics at Knox College in Trunk City, Alberta.

3:30 "Collage" continues. The fourth part of this afternoon's program will include *Ludus Macaronicus,* a twelfth-century music drama in Latin and Manx, for five countertenors and shawm, realised by Desmond Bilboes; *Friar John and the Emperor's Courtesan,* excerpts from the 12,000-line *geste d'amour,* translated by Roy Ketchum; and Dom Anselmo Jodl's reconstruction of the three-voice conductus *Non sunt impotentes omnes monachi, alleluia* from the St. Magdalene Troper of the Little Sisters of Gramercy.

BEFORE THEY INTERVIEWED Arnold Gloss, Inspector Coggin had a man assigned, a Sergeant Furbelow, to call on Mrs. Casement and check on whatever part of her husband's story she could confirm or not, as the case might be. He wished he had a woman to assign, since the situation was of a delicacy that would only be magnified by the natural reticence that hampers any attempt at intimate conversation between a man and a woman who have not previously met. However, the department had not seen fit, as yet, to post a policewoman to his unit, even for training, on the curious grounds that no woman was strong enough. He had been unable to convince his superiors that having the strength to carry out an arrest, in a homicide, was much less necessary than having the brains to find out whom to arrest; and, to his despair, the only administrator who could comprehend this point immediately replied that women were per se, unsuitable because logic was a faculty of the masculine mind.[1] Overruled, he had to make do with the

[1] The administrator who said this would not have been pleased if the illogic of his own position had been pointed out. For the same tradition that excluded women from the homicide squad, because they lack muscle,

9

personnel he was given: most of whom, granted, were good men; but he wished, at times like this, that things could be otherwise. Meanwhile, Sergeant Furbelow, who was stout and gentle and reassuring, could be counted on to do as good a job as any male could.[2]

Arnold Gloss, who had come to the CBC from the advertising firm of Gowdy, Amussi, Jitter, was everything Miss Vulpitude had predicted—and more. His sharkskin suit was adroitly modish without being insufferable; his hair came trimly down to his collar, at the exact length to reassure both young and old; his digital watch, when not called upon for a read-out, presented to the world a face as blank as a starter's cartridge; and his attitude to people was like plasticine, willing to adopt whatever shape might please. He was born in a small Ontario town called Bowman's Corners, and had grown up yearning for the glamour (as he saw it) of big-city life. Since then, he had never stopped trying to catch up with his own aspirations—a pursuit forever fruitless, seemingly, for every step towards his immediate goal extended his horizon, revealed a further goal of greater glamour and sophistication to aim at. Fresh out of business school, he hit Toronto in the nineteen-fifties, eager for the role of fashionable bachelor-about-town, complete with Austin Healey, hi-fi, and an apartment with bamboo curtains. The sixties had seen him move on, smoothly, to marriage and a split-level in the more expensive section of Don Mills. Now, in the seventies, he was ready for divorce and a chic townhouse on a renovated cul-de-sac in the city core. Nothing was left in him of Bowman's Corners except the second syllable of *about*, which endured on his tongue as a triphthong, and occasionally, late at night and alone with his final scotch, a desolating sense

---

sent them out on street duty, where muscle is often needed. Most murderers surrender meekly; but violence, on the beat, is commonplace.

[2] Ironically, he was forty-five pounds overweight, and demonstrably less fit than the famous sixty-five-year-old Swedish grandmother: if he had had to arrest a violent and strong suspect, he would have been as ineffectual as the helpless female of Victorian myth and Police Department tradition.

of loss if he confronted some jarring reminder, in a movie perhaps, of what it means to have had roots once and to be
severed from them. This he shared with no one and rebuffed,
as best he could, from himself.

Today, joining Inspector Coggin and Sergeant Sump, he was
in every respect what Miss Vulpitude had forecast, suavely
soothing this corporate loss into the decorous rituals of public
grief. There was, however, something extra which she had not,
and could not have, foreseen: a tension, a forcing of the glib
hypocrisies, so that they sounded vaguely hollow instead of
bearing their customary freight of ninety-proof sincerity. It was
as though he were going through the obligatory motions of glu-
cose tribute, without putting his heart into it—and, as every
salesman knows, it is not enough to merely have your pitch
down pat: you have to seem to be meaning what you say. And
salesmanship, in this, is not unlike the making of mayonnaise,
which, if it, too, is to whet the appetite as intended, requires
not only flair but also an unremitting attentiveness, and the
least declension from either spells ruin.

"Yes," he was saying, "Henry Midden was a figure to be
reckoned with. His place in the annals of our broadcasting system is secure. We cannot hope, in our time, to see his like
again."

Inspector Coggin could not help noticing that this affecting
memorial did not expressly state what virtues, if any, Mr. Midden would be remembered for. Indeed, it left open the question of whether it was, in fact, for his virtues or for his vices
that the man would be remembered; and he wondered if this
ambivalence might be, consciously or unconsciously, deliberate.
It reminded him of the devastating ambiguity with which a
music critic some years ago, reviewing a recital by a singer
whose appearance in public owed more to pull than to talent,
had remarked that she possessed a voice "of a quality seldom
heard upon the concert stage."

Sergeant Sump, however, could not afford the luxury of such
reflections. He was pressing on with the next question. "Would

you say," he asked, "that Mr. Midden had any enemies among his close associates?"

Gloss stiffened, like a mortician hearing a loud joke in a funeral parlour. "Really, Sergeant," he countered, "I do think that's a rather tasteless suggestion. He was, after all, one of our more eminent executives."

There was a moment's pause, in which Inspector Coggin wondered if this dulcet epitaph was offered as an automatic proof of sainthood; but then the qualification followed.

"Mind you," Gloss went on, "I don't suppose everyone always agreed one hundred per cent with every least thing he did. In that sense, there will have been differences. But real enmity, no. Certainly not on a level of violence. I do hope you're not suggesting that one of *us* might have . . ." His voice, bleating like a saccharinely played oboe, trailed off into the silence of the unspeakable. And his hands, as though he saw that unspeakable thought in apparition before him, made a small pushing gesture in the air, in front of his chest.

"Well, sir," Sergeant Sump replied, "we have to assume something; we can't just let it go. Let's put it this way: you leave the tasteless suggestions to us; and if none of 'em stand up, no one'll be more pleased than me. Okay? Right. Now, it looks to us as though Mr. Midden was killed by someone who knew him. And presumably there was a motive, either private or professional. So let's look at the professional possibilities for a moment. And there really are only two that are at all likely: either he was killed because somebody hated him; or else because he stood in somebody's way. Well, I'll be frank with you: if somebody hated him enough to kill him, the chances are that hatred was all bottled up inside and we won't find any clues lying around to tell us who it might be; so if that's it, we'll just have to hope we'll be lucky enough to stumble across some leads. But if he was killed out of ambition, that's something we can investigate in a systematic way. And the obvious place to begin is by finding out who might be in line for his job. Maybe somebody figures his chances would be good if he struck right now, but not so good if he waited till Mr. Midden retired."

"But surely, Sergeant," Gloss protested, "nobody'd be dumb enough to run that kind of risk simply for a promotion? After all, you're talking about intelligent people."

Sergeant Sump was briefly tempted to borrow from Norm Casement and reply "Bullshit!" However, he did not wish as yet to interrupt the syrupy flow of their discourse: shock was too often useful as a tactic for him to waste it on an impulse. So he replied, unargumentatively, "Maybe. But I'm also suggesting one of those intelligent people may have become unbalanced. Sure, I agree, no fully rational man would do a thing like that. But ambition does strange things to a person sometimes. You never know. So I'd certainly appreciate it if you could give me a run-down on who the people might be that we're talking about."

Gloss did not seem to find this request at all disconcerting. Indeed, it clearly flattered his vanity to be consulted. He pondered the matter sagaciously and with detachment, as though he had been asked which rank of bureaucrat might be allowed plushier carpets in the annual divvying up of operational funds. And Sergeant Sump noticed in him, at this point, a relaxation, as though some inner pressure (or even fear) had been relieved: the manner was no longer tense, as it had been hitherto, or preoccupied.

"Basically," Gloss said, "there are two lists of viable candidates" (Inspector Coggin flinched at this fashionable misusage: it belonged with *parameters* and *chauvinist* in the flaccid corpus of vogue inaccuracy): "the local ones, and the ones out in the regions." He then proceeded to list the same Toronto executives as had already been listed more than once that day, "including" with a small, sick smile "myself: it would be false modesty to pretend otherwise." And his out-of-town list was the same as the list in Henry Midden's memo, as was his dismissiveness of their qualifications: they were almost all, in his view, lightweights. The one exception was Bill Hoyle, of

Vancouver, "and you certainly couldn't describe him as a light-weight. But I can't really think he'd be a serious candidate, either: he's blotted his copybook too often with Upper Management. Mind you, the producers'd love it if he got the job: half the trouble he's ever had was because he went to bat for program ideas when the Administration had more important things to consider. But that's why he was sent out to the coast, so I doubt if he'd have anything more than an outside chance."

Inspector Coggin had several relatives in Saskatchewan who regarded him as the black sheep of the family for having come East. He usually regarded prejudice of this sort as the mark of an immature mind. But every now and then he came across incidents or attitudes which did seem, to some extent, to justify western paranoia. And certainly, if the CBC regarded British Columbia as a useful Siberia to which to exile wayward executives, there might be some grounds for Vancouver's notoriously vitriolic xenophobia.

Sergeant Sump's musings were rather more pertinent to the matter at hand. He already had a request out for a checkup on each of the possible out-of-town suspects, on where they had been last night. In the case of Bill Hoyle, he decided to ask for a double-check: here, possibly, was a man in whom there had been combined the two motives of ambition and revenge. Meanwhile, there'd be no harm in trying to get a handle on him. "Tell me about this Mr. Hoyle," he said. "What sort of a guy is he? Do you know him?"

"Oh yes, known him for years: he was head of Features, here, till they sent him out West in seventy-six." Gloss paused, casting about in his mind, perhaps, for the judicious words and tone of voice with which to convey his unenthusiasm for Hoyle without seeming to be inimical. He decided, evidently, that condescension would be the right tack. "A gentleman," he said, "but a gentleman of the old school. He hasn't kept up with the times, and I imagine a good part of his frustration is the feeling that the world's passing him by. For instance, four years ago, when we cancelled 'CBC Friday Night,' he did everything he could to oppose us, short of resigning. We all thought it was rather uncalled for, since that series was mostly music or drama and hardly ever features, so he really didn't have any stake in it himself; but he kept on griping away as though that sort of thing were the end of the world. In fact, after a while he became quite hysterical about it—accused us of turning the AM Network into a cultural wasteland. And there's good reason to believe he was behind the campaign of letters to the newspapers complaining we were putting ratings ahead of quality— we didn't have an easy time defusing that, I can tell you." Gloss sighed over the memory of it: his right to use the editorial *we* was small consolation for the trouble he was sometimes put to.

Inspector Coggin joined in the train of reminiscence. "Wasn't there once a program called 'CBC Thursday Night' like that?" he asked. "Mostly drama and music?"

"Yes, it was the same series," Gloss replied. "We just changed the night it was on. Same kind of élitist content, experts talking to experts, and no concern for the average listener's tastes: nobody out in the boondocks appreciates that kind of stuff. For a tenth the budget we could have pulled in ten times the audience by putting on a phone-in and getting people really involved. But you try telling that to a stick-in-the-mud like Bill Hoyle: he doesn't seem to realise we've entered the age of participatory broadcasting; the audience of tomorrow is the disco generation, and what listeners want today is Personalities." He sighed again: years of stuffy culture had made it hard for him to sell the corporation to the public as a With It outfit.

"Meanwhile," enquired the inspector, "what happened to Bach?"

"Who?"

"Bach. J. S. Bach."

"Oh yes, Bach." Gloss recovered his cheery poise, his affability towards all tastes however odd. "Well, of course, we hope there'll always be a place for Serious Music in our schedule. We owe that to Canada's many thousands of devoted music lovers. Though I think you'll agree that Bach's a fairly sophisticated diet. All very well for FM listeners, but a little goes a long way on our AM stations. What's needed there is a very careful choice of host, to help put it across."

It was the inspector's turn to sigh. "I suppose I have to leave that to you fellows, as the experts in the business," he observed drily. "Though I must say when I learnt to love Bach, as a farm boy growing up in Saskatchewan, it was by listening to him on one of your AM stations; and in those days they didn't play the finale of a concerto without the first two movements and describe it as a 'delightful selection' or some such drivel." He stopped short. "Sorry, it's quite beside the point what *I* think. And I'm sure it isn't your fault anyway."

Arnold Gloss was not a P.R. man for nothing: gracefully and in two sentences, he accepted the inspector's apology and passed the ball back to Sergeant Sump. "There you have it, Sergeant," he exclaimed: "you were asking me about Bill Hoyle and there you have it, the gospel according to Hoyle; Hoyle's viewpoint eloquently expressed by the inspector himself, and I couldn't have done it better myself. It's not a view which I happen to share but, as the inspector just said, it's quite beside the point what *I* think."

Sergeant Sump decided it might be best, in the circumstances, to add his two-bits' worth of amiability to the prevailing weather, but to proceed without more delay to his unexpected thrust. "Well, I wouldn't exactly say that, Mr. Gloss," he commented. "I'm sure at your level of responsibility everybody's opinion is given a good deal of weight."

Gloss smiled, all defences down.

"By the way," Sergeant Sump continued, "after the meeting last night, what were you and Mr. Midden fighting about?"

To his surprise, and to the inspector's embarrassment, the man burst into tears.

What followed, when Gloss eventually gained some measure of control, was a halting recitation of misery and squalor utterly at odds with the debonair image he presented to the

world. He had stayed behind last evening, he said, because
Midden had asked him to, in connection with business. "But
that was only a pretext. Fact was, why he wanted me there was
he wanted to beef at me. About Cynthia—that's my wife. You
see, things haven't been right for a long time now between she
and I."

The inspector cringed: grief and solecism are confounding
partners.

Gloss enlarged on the point. Maritally, he'd been impotent
for the last five years. This had made his wife easy prey for se-
duction; and Midden had seized the chance when it came his
way. About six months ago. "But the trouble was it didn't
mean anything—to him. I guess it was just another of his passing flings. Cynthia, though, she got obsessed by it—almost as
bad as an addict needing his fixes: she just had to get laid. By
Henry. And that's what Henry's beef was: said she was all the
time bugging him, and he was fed up."

Sergeant Sump could well imagine this. It's a common char-
acteristic of philanderers to tire quickly of every latest con-
quest.

"He said she wasn't his type," Gloss went on dolefully.
"Know what he called her? 'The titless wonder.' Christ, some
people just don't care how a person might feel." He sniffed,
and blew his nose. "As a matter of fact I can remember his
exact words. He said, 'For God's sake, Arnold, I've told her a
hundred times to get off my back. I no more want to shack up
with her than I do with anyone else: it gets boring plowing the
same furrow all the time. Can't you keep her home and screw
her yourself? She's pretty good, you know.' Just like that."

It was then, out of the blue, that Bowman's Corners had
come to the rescue of Arnold Gloss. Ordinarily, civility leashed
his tongue and timidity his ire. But just this once, suddenly,
stress had suspended these restraints. Lacking any habitual
fund of vituperative rejoinder, at least in his current life style,
he had heard himself, with some astonishment, cursing Henry
Midden out with the accent and vocabulary of a small-town

zoot-suiter from twenty years ago. He had long ago eliminated these strains from his discourse: they too readily disclosed a social origin he was ashamed of, and the modern fad for sprinkling the coarser expletives into polite conversation made him uneasy; he didn't feel he could pull it off with the authentic air of condescension worn by those who make amused visits to the cultural slums. And slums they were, in his memory: every week, aged fifteen, he had gone on Saturday night pilgrimage five miles up the road to Cy's Billiards and Tastee Snax, in Haunch End, for pool and pilfered cigarettes and profanity; he had put all this behind him, he thought, for keeps. But now the profanity poured out of him, fluent with deep grudge, acrimonious, shrill as a band saw. He relished every moment of it and brought it to a raucous, purgative conclusion.

There had been a moment's silence. And then Henry Midden, totally unperturbed, had grinned, chuckled, and finally laughed in his face. "Jesus, Arnold," he'd said, "I never knew you had that much spunk in you. Well, I tell you what: I hate to spoil a good marriage, or for that matter our own working relationship; so here's what we'll do. You go home to Cynthia and stick it to her a bit more often, eh? And if it's going to make everybody happy, you can tell her to give me a call once a month and come on over. How's about it?"

He had tried to resummon, desperately, that vanished teenager he had once been, who had come so unaccountably to his rescue a minute beforehand. But the ghost had gone, irretrievable by mere wishing in this his further hour of need. The best he'd been able to manage had been to say, lamely, "You know something, Henry, you're a rotten bastard"; and then he had heard Norm Casement using the phone in the outer office, and said "Oh shit!" and broke the conversation off.

At this point his recital petered out, and Sergeant Sump resumed the questioning. Gloss corroborated that he'd gotten a ride home with Norm Casement—and added, voluntarily, "But I didn't come back downtown with a tire iron and beat Henry to death, if that's what you're thinking. Though I wish I had."

"Can you verify that, Mr. Gloss?" the sergeant asked. "I mean, is there anyone who can bear out what you say, that you got home and stayed home?"

"Well, there's always Norm," he replied. "He can tell you I got home all right. And you could ask Cynthia: she'd probably back me up, at least that far."

"Yes, but even so, that only proves you got there. It doesn't prove you stayed there." Sergeant Sump shifted uncomfortably. "Mr. Gloss, this is kind of embarrassing to ask, but in the circumstances I have to. Do you and your wife sleep together?" He amended himself awkwardly. "I mean, do you share the same bedroom?"

The sergeant's evident discomfort had the effect of putting Gloss substantially more at ease, which was exactly what the Sergeant had intended. He replied, more composedly, "No, we don't. So I guess that eliminates her as a witness. But still, I think I am able to make a case for myself. You see, I couldn't sleep, so I stayed up for a couple of hours. And I didn't have anything better to do, so I watched the late show on CBC-TV. If you want me to, I daresay I could give you a fairly detailed account of it, which I could hardly do if I hadn't watched it. And then I can certainly prove I was still there at two-thirty, because that's when my stepdaughter got home. She'd been out on a date, and she came in and said good night to me before going to bed."

These recollections seemed about to bring on another bout of lachrymose ululation: his sinuses clogged up with dolor, and his voice quavered like an oboe in full bleat. He choked, and asked if that would do for now; and they allowed that yes for now it would. But before he left to go elsewhere, they requested him to dictate a statement to the police typist in the outer office, detailing what he had seen on the late-night show. Then they excused him. He stumbled out of the room, bedraggled and forlorn. Inspector Coggin turned to his colleague and shook his head sympathetically. "Poor little bugger!" he said. "Do you buy it?"

Sergeant Sump nodded. "Oh sure. A guy like that wouldn't put himself down the way he did if it wasn't genuine."

"I know," the inspector replied. "But what I meant was, do you buy his alibi?"

"Probably. We can check his statement later against the actual content of the late show, but I shan't be surprised if they agree. Besides, guilty people usually have a better alibi than that handy, with witnesses. At least, they do if there's any kind of premeditation."

"Yes, but that's the whole point, Fred," the inspector said. "There may have been plenty of provocation for a premeditated murder. But the way he told it, if he did do it, it was more likely on the spur of the moment. If so, it'd make sense for him not to have a perfect alibi. Then again, even if it was premeditated, that's just the sort of alibi he'd come up with if he's astute: it's far more important for an alibi to sound like real life than for it to be a hundred per cent watertight; and this chap's a P.R. man, so he presumably understands what sort of stories people will go for. We should know. Remember Max?"

Indeed Sergeant Sump did remember Max—Maxwell Tidy, their near-nemesis. He was the alibi artist par excellence, simply by virtue of being plausible rather than excessively complete. A mild little accountant with rimless glasses and an inoffensive manner, he had sliced his wife up into seventy-four small, easily packaged pieces, which he stored in his deep freeze and disposed of, over the next thirty-seven weeks, by putting them out one at a time in his twice-weekly garbage. His alibi for the day of her disappearance was utterly convincing: it involved, allegedly, an abduction. He and his wife had picked up a couple of hitchhikers, who promptly pulled a gun on him and forced him to drive out into the country, near Peyer's Patch. There they had pushed him out of the car, first relieving him of his wallet with all his cash in it, and had then driven off with his wife still in the car as a hostage. He had made his way up the road to the police station in Belcher, and reported the incident; and the next day the car was found abandoned, out of gas, on a back road in Bone County. No trace of his wife was found, or of the hitchhikers. Yet nobody disbelieved his story. There were no supporting witnesses, but his account of the abduction was embellished with such a wealth of purely gratuitous and odd detail, of a kind that would not normally occur to anyone except the Dickensian kind of novelist, that everyone who heard it gave it credence; and this evidence solidified when his account remained consistent under repeated interrogation. In consequence, the physical investigation was not as thorough as it should have been, and the neatly wrapped parcels of meat in Mr. Tidy's freezer had not been opened and examined. His wife was put on the Missing Persons list, and the case stagnated.

There, probably, it would have ended, except that in the very last week of his disposal project the murderer got unlucky. Each garbage collection day he waited until the garbage truck appeared at the end of the street before putting his garbage out. This eliminated the risk that his garbage might be ripped open by a stray dog or a raccoon and the contents exposed, if he put it out earlier; then, that done, he would leave for work. On the seventy-fourth such day, when he was disposing of the last package, he followed this pattern as usual, and went off to work with a quiet, triumphant mind. So he was totally unaware that three houses up the road one of the garbagemen had a heart attack and his mates put him in the truck and drove hell for leather to the hospital, where incidentally he survived. This left Mr. Tidy's garbage still at the edge of his lot and exactly what he had feared did in fact happen: a vagrant Airedale tore it apart and ripped open the various packages, including the crucial one. And there sitting on the sidewalk for all to see, not in the least decomposed after nine weeks in the deep freeze, was the head of the late Mrs. Tidy. Inspector Coggin and Sergeant Sump admitted, grudgingly, that in Max the world had probably lost a great master of fiction. But the memory of their duping was not a happy one.

Sergeant Sump's mind returned to the case at hand. "Here's the problem," he said. "He may have told us a story to fit one kind of crime, while actually having committed another kind. What I mean is, suppose he killed Midden with premeditation; then he tells us the sort of story that points to a spur-of-the-moment killing, and he backs it up with the sort of alibi that genuinely would be told by an innocent man with the same story. It's not beyond the bounds of human ingenuity. Not after Max. Nothing is. But how do you figure it out?"

"On evidence," the inspector replied, characteristically. "Admittedly, there isn't much to go on, yet. But we can make a start. For instance, the late show—he'd better not make any errors there."

"Don't count on it, Andrew. I saw the first bit of it myself; it was a movie, *The Case of the Gargling Gumshoe*, with Flint Carver." Sergeant Sump blushed again; he knew his superior did not approve of these excursions into the cultural slums of detective romance. "If it had been a talk show, he'd have had to watch it to know what went on. But a well-known movie, he could have seen it when it was around in the theatres: if he has a good memory, he'd remember enough of what was in it. And as for knowing what the commercials were, presumably a CBC executive like him has easy access to that kind of information, on his own station. So maybe we won't be any further ahead anyway."

"Maybe." Inspector Coggin was willing to wait and see. "But the commercials could be the key. Movies are cut to shreds when they're shown on television, to fit the commercials in. So if he describes a scene from remembering it in the theatre, and it turns out that that scene was cut in last night's screening, we know he's lying. You'd better arrange for the cut version to be held, so we can compare."

Sergeant Sump went out to Miss Vulpitude's office to see that this was done.

NINE

Tuesday, 4:00–4:30

PROGRAM SCHEDULE #8: 4:00–4:30

4:00 News

4:04 "Yours Truly" (till six o'clock), with Darryl Hayhoe:
music to drive home by, weather reports, and chitchat.
Guests in the first half hour will be Lukas Grabchick,
chairman of the Ontario government committee on the
Status of Women; Mildred Spratt, with a new recipe for
fishburgers; and Lefty Czerwinski, the famous pitcher,
who has just co-authored his autobiography, with Luther
Bucket, under the title *Strike Out!*

4:00 "Whither Academe?" a round-table discussion from
Bluenose University in Blind Head, Cape Breton: with
Professor Oxytone, Dr. Hypotenuse, and Dean Slide, re-
spectively of the classics, mathematics, and engineering
departments; chairman, Darius T. Pugwash. Production,
H. B. Strudwick.

WAITING HIS TURN outside in Miss Vulpitude's office was Bud Benedict; and when Sergeant Sump went back into the inner office, he accompanied him. His mood was dour: he had spent the afternoon listening to tapes of three programs in his Ecology series (*Slurry*, a portrait of industrial neglect, by Emory Pebble; *Elijah Crust*, the forgotten man of sewage recycling, by Spencer Forbes; and *Waste Not Want Not*, an in-depth study of manure, by Diana Schütz). It was not often that he subjected himself to the fare he inflicted on listeners, for he shared with small children and lapsed religious the view that good works, while perhaps obligatory, are definitely tedious. The prospect of a police grilling had done little to improve his humour.

"Mr. Benedict," Inspector Coggin began, "when did you last see Henry Midden?"

He considered, and spoke. All his utterances had about them a flavour of unabashed magniloquence: he had lived for years off his voice, which commanded attention and caressed the ear, irrespective of what was being said.[1] His critics, however,

[1] In this he resembled a certain famous actor, necessarily nameless here, who is endowed with one of the great voices of our time and lazily relies

averred that any speech by Bud Benedict was living refutation of the theory that nature abhors a vacuum. What he said now, in a tone altogether too grandiose for the triviality of the content, was: "About quarter to eleven last night. We had an evening meeting down here, several of us, and that's when it broke up." He paused, in a practised manner, drawing attention to what he would say next. "However, that wasn't the last time I heard from him. It only takes me about ten minutes to drive home, and just after I walked in the door he phoned me."

Inspector Coggin was not experienced in the role of a straight man, so his timing was a little off. But he did manage to deliver himself of the awkward question. "Do you think you could tell us what he called about?"

"Oh certainly." Benedict was all compliance, bass-baritone and sostenuto. "He said this was something to be between ourselves, which he hadn't wanted to bring up at the meeting: namely, he'd like me to prepare a report on how well my department was being served by the Public Relations people. What that meant in translation, if I knew Henry, was that he wanted a *bad* report, so he could do a hatchet job on Arnold Gloss—he's our head of P.R."

Sergeant Sump: "That's very interesting. Had you had any reason to expect a request like that?"

"No, as a matter of fact I hadn't. It took me quite by surprise. Arnold's the kind of guy who just doesn't get into trouble; sort of Dale Carnegie type."

"Yes, we've met him."

"But then," Benedict went on, "you never did know who Henry might dump on next. Working under him was like signing on with Idi Amin: precarious, you might say." He paused again, confident of their heed. "From which you may gather

---

on the spell it can cast over audiences, thus saving himself the trouble of creating a complete or authentic performance. In Bud Benedict's case, such reliance could be forgiven, since he possessed no other talents and little intellect. In the case of the star alluded to, forgiveness is less readily meted out, for he has enormous natural talent as an actor, which he neglects; and even after years of abusing it with drunkenness, possesses one of the finest minds in the business.

that our late general manager was not about to win a popularity contest. But I'm sure, if you've been on the case since this morning, that won't be exactly news to you."

"No, we did rather gain that impression," Inspector Coggin responded. "Now, Mr. Benedict, I wonder if we could just go over a few small points with you—straightforward things, points of fact, little details only you might know." And he proceeded to cover again the ground gone over before with the other witnesses: who was at the meeting; what had been discussed; whether there had been anything unusual in the air; who had left when. The answers all agreed with what they already knew.

Sergeant Sump took over. "And after you'd finished talking to Mr. Midden on the phone, what did you do then?"

The pause which followed this question had nothing whatever to do with rhetorical habit: it was purely spontaneous, and unsettled—his timing had been thrown off. And the voice when it emerged was no longer the confident diapason of a cathedral organ: rather, the uncertain creak of a parish harmonium, tentatively pumped. "I er . . . I went out . . . to visit a friend."

This was followed, uncharacteristically, by a lame silence. Sergeant Sump had to prompt: "And?"

"And I got home quite late, I guess."

Another silence.

"Mr. Benedict," the sergeant said, "I'm afraid you'll have to give us a bit more detail than that. Naturally, anything you tell us will remain in confidence unless it has a bearing on the case. But we do have to know."

"All right." The man's air was at once desperate and furtive. Little remained of the voice that had riveted Canada from coast to coast with play-by-play accounts of quilting bees, reports from the opening ceremonies of municipal reservoirs, and colour-commentary on the grafting of hybrid plums. He was diminished. "What do you want to know?"

Question after question, they dragged it out of him, answer

following upon answer with increasing reluctance and embarrassment, but finally with a kind of dreary resignation. How he had had a date with a boy friend . . .

"A boy friend, Mr. Benedict?"

"Well, not exactly. A male prostitute, actually." Pressed for details, he named the modelling agency the boy worked for.

Sergeant Sump: "I take it, then, that Mister Peter's is more than just a modelling agency. Does double duty as a homosexual brothel, eh?"

"That's right."

"On the premises?"

"No, of course not." Benedict recovered himself almost to the point of allowing a sneer to come into his voice: dumb questions were evidently somewhat reassuring. Sergeant Sump had meant him to feel reassured.

"Where, then?"

"At Alistair's apartment."

They dragged the address out of him: a luxury apartment well west of town, among the Oakville millionaires. It was leased in the tenant's own name, which he gave them; and no, Alistair was *not* a minor.

"And when did you arrive there?"

"About midnight, give or take a few minutes."

"And how long were you there?"

"A bit longer than . . ." he hesitated; "than usual. I was going to leave after . . . er . . . after a while, but we got to talking. And I could hardly believe it, but Alistair actually tried to blackmail me."

"How?" Sergeant Sump could always tell when a witness was starting to unravel. At such times, only the most vestigial prompting was needed.

"Oh really, Sergeant, I'm sure you don't need me to tell you the facts of life. You know perfectly well that people of my sexual identity are easy targets. Society hasn't accepted us that much, yet. In private maybe, some of the time. And I guess in the theatre. But certainly not in positions of public trust. All he'd have to do would be squeal on me to our top brass, and that'd be it."

"He knew who you were, then?"

"Certainly he did." Benedict came as close to pouting as his generally unqueenlike demeanour would allow. "It's not the same with us as it is in the straight world. From what I can gather, sex with a woman prostitute is simply *functional:* no genuine relationship, no tenderness. Well, I'm happy to say we don't sink quite that low. That's why I was so shocked: I thought we meant something to each other. So yes, of course he knew who I was. In fact, he knew more than that: he knew who to go to if it ever did come to blowing the gaff on me: Henry Midden."

"How d'you think he figured that?"

"He didn't. It landed in his lap, so to speak. Apparently Henry had some kind of 'in' with the agency. Used to come around from time to time and screw the boss."

For the first time that day Sergeant Sump was incredulous. "Henry Midden? With Mister Peter?"

Benedict sniggered unpleasantly. "It's all right, Sergeant. Henry wasn't one of our converts. Mister Peter is actually a very attractive forty-year-old lady. Very reliable person except for that one thing: seems she'd give her right arm for Henry. No accounting for tastes, is there? Anyway, he just *used* her, of course. And from what Alistair told me, I understand Henry had some kind of standing order with her, that if any of her boys had clients in his bailiwick, the information was to be funnelled back to him. Typical piece of Henry: never miss a chance to ferret out the dirt on people—more power over them that way."

"So what did you do? I mean, when the young fellow laid this on you?"

"Do? Nothing. At least, not right away. I told Alistair I'd think it over and maybe see him later in the week. Then I left."

"When was that, Mr. Benedict?"

"Oh, about two-thirty, I should think."

"And?"

Benedict paused. "I went home."

"Straight home?"

"No, not straight home, actually. Actually, I didn't get in till about half-past three."

Sergeant Sump proceeded to ask, as he so often had to, the obvious. "And what were you doing between two-thirty and half-past three?"

Benedict looked at him with a face full of wretchedness and defeat. His reply was no longer fragmentary or piecemeal, but continuous, an unburdening, and delivered in a hopeless monotone:

"I was here. I hadn't meant to come here, but I go by on the way home; and I saw the light on in Henry's office. Well, I knew he sometimes worked weird hours, and it occurred to me, if he was in, the sensible thing to do would be to go in and see him and tell him straight out the fix I was in. At least it would be better than being blackmailed. And I doubt if I'd get fired over it: they couldn't really afford to fire me on those grounds, with one of our vice-presidents in exactly the same boat; especially considering *his* case involved sixteen-year-olds."

Sergeant Sump felt that the conversation was in danger of being diverted to side issues. He steered it back on course. "So you came by here and saw Mr. Midden's lights on. Can you say at all accurately when that was?"

"Yes, as a matter of fact I can. Seeing his lights on like that at such a late hour made me wonder just what time it was, so I looked at my watch. It was five past three."

"Right. Now please describe what happened then."

Benedict shifted uncomfortably in his chair. "I parked on the street, right outside the front door. The back door is left unlocked for the night staff; but I have a key to the front door, and I let myself in. As I was doing so, I heard someone going out the back door and shutting it behind him—not that I thought anything of it at the time. So I went in to Miss Vulpitude's office to come on through into here. The lights were off in her office, but plenty of light came in from the hallway and I could see where I was heading. The door into here was ajar and the room was pitch dark. I called out "Henry!" and there wasn't any answer. So I just assumed he'd switched the lights out and left while I was getting the key out and letting myself in, and that when I had come in the front door it was him I heard going out the back."

He paused briefly. "I suppose I ought to have gone after him and called him back. But somehow I couldn't. It wasn't exactly pleasant, what I'd screwed my nerve up to do. And when he wasn't there, it was like being let off. For the time being, anyway. I knew I'd have to go through with it eventually."

Again a pause, then: "Of course, when I heard the news this morning, I realised that the person I heard leaving may very well have been the murderer. If I'd come a couple of minutes earlier I would have run into him—or even caught him in the act." He grimaced at the thought, and added wearily: "I realise too, of course, that what I've said makes me a prime suspect: simply by being here just then. Except, if I did kill Henry, I'd have had to kill Alistair, too, to protect myself. And if you enquire, I daresay you'll find he's alive and well and living in clover, the rotten little bastard."

"Well, we will have to check this out with him. Do you think he'll confirm your leaving at two o'clock?"

Benedict sighed. "I don't see why he wouldn't. Though I suppose you'll think his sort isn't a very reliable witness. And I can't say I'd blame you. Up till last night I used to think I could trust him. I sure know better now."

Inspector Coggin took the cue from his colleague: the questioning was now in his territory. "And how about your arrival here at five past three?" he asked. "I don't suppose there's anyone can corroborate that."

"Not so far as I know. I'm not aware that anyone saw me coming or going. But if you try driving it, you'll find it takes about that long to get from Alistair's place to here, at that time of night."

"And when you left here, what then?"

"Oh, I drove around for a few minutes, to cool off—I was pretty tense, you understand. Then I just went home, and went to bed."

"Any corroboration of that?"

"Yes. My wife woke up when I crawled in, and asked me what time it was."

Inspector Coggin was annoyed with himself for feeling surprised. Lots of queers have wives, he remembered: it's nothing to feel shocked about, even if it is incomprehensible. He redirected his thoughts, away from the puzzling quagmire of emotion, back to the solid ground of behaviour. "Earlier on," he said, "you left your place after talking to Mr. Midden on the phone and arrived at . . . er . . . Alistair's around midnight. Any corroboration of that?"

"Well, if Alistair'll confirm my leaving at two, he'll probably confirm my arriving at midnight. I hope so, anyway. And as far as leaving my place is concerned, yes: I ran into the super in the lobby, on the way out, and we had a chat about one of the elevators that was being repaired."

"Okay, we'll check that out too. And I guess that about wraps it up for now. Was there anything more you wanted to ask, Sergeant?"

"No, I don't think so." Sergeant Sump leaned back, kindly and sympathetic. "Mr. Benedict," he said, "I want you to know we appreciate your being so frank with us. I'm sure it wasn't easy for you."

Benedict looked at him gratefully. "Thanks," he said. "Still, I can't make a virtue out of necessity. I mean, I had to come clean, didn't I? I've no means of knowing whether anyone saw me here at three o'clock. And if someone did, it'd have looked pretty bad for me if I hadn't explained it to you myself first, wouldn't it? Especially as you were pretty well bound to have found out I'd gone out last night, with the super being right there." He paused, and changed the subject. "Look, I know it's early yet. But if you do catch the murderer, does this other business have to come out?"

"Not necessarily. Not if it has no direct bearing. But I do advise you to do something about it, though. That young man can be charged with attempted blackmail if you lay a complaint against him. I wish more people like him did get charged: I've seen far too much human tragedy come out of situations like that, and it isn't necessary, you know. However, that'll have to be up to you."

Benedict hesitated, and Sergeant Sump sensed then that he probably wouldn't in fact take that difficult step. At the moment he had other worries. "But aside from that, Sergeant, there wouldn't actually be any charges, eh?"

"Oh, you mean against you? No, not that I can see. Prostitution isn't a crime, nor is patronising a prostitute: only soliciting. And it doesn't sound to me as though there was any soliciting involved. Just so long as your young man is over the age of eighteen, which according to the Ontario government defines him as an adult. And, as our great and good King Shrug has proclaimed, what happens in private between consenting adults is no business of the law's. Mind you, you fellows are the real beneficiaries of that pronouncement. Female prostitutes still get pretty short shrift."

"Maybe. But at least in the straight world you don't have to be afraid of prejudice." A peevish note was creeping into Benedict's voice, the first sign of reviving confidence now that the strain of his confession was over, a prelude to the return of his normal orotundity. "After all, if you want to be fair, straight people do have all the advantages. The best I could hope for was not to be found out. But a woman can get ahead just by being a woman, and don't you let Women's Lib tell you any different. Up with the skirt and down with the panties, and hey presto the job's yours. Happens all the time. Especially around an old lecher like Henry Midden. For instance, you ask Joyce Parchment how she got her promotion."

Sergeant Sump was saddened. He had felt sorry for Benedict, to some extent; but now, with this display of bitchiness, his compassion evaporated. "Joyce Parchment? Your FM director?"

"Yes."

"Well, maybe we will ask her. But while you're here, Mr. Benedict, why don't you give us your version?"

"My version? It's not a question of my version. It's just a simple case of putting two and two together and coming up with the obvious. She's gorgeous-looking, if you like a woman built like a cow (which I gather Henry did); and she isn't qualified. So why else would she get the position?"

"I daresay we'll find out, sir, one way or another, before very long." Sergeant Sump recognised the pure malice in what he had just heard, which he found deeply obnoxious, and he took due note of the light it cast on the man's character. But he was also willing to listen to real evidence, if there was any. So he added, "Mind you, there isn't much to go on in what you suggest. Do you have anything concrete you base it on? Anything you can vouch for yourself?"

"Not if you mean did I catch them at it with my own two eyes, no I didn't," Benedict said sulkily. "But what does it matter anyway? We all know that sort of thing's perfectly acceptable all the time in the straight world."

If he expected an argument, he didn't get one. And on that awkward note the interview ended.

Sergeant Sump shook his head with disrelish as the door closed. "Jesus," he said, "that kind of thing leaves a bad taste in your mouth, doesn't it? I'm not sure I want to see this Parchment lady right away, after that."

Unheeding, the intercom spoke up, in the voice of Miss Vulpitude: "Mrs. Parchment to see you," it said.

145

TEN

Tuesday, 4:30–5:00

PROGRAM SCHEDULE #9: 4:30–5:00

4:30 "Yours Truly" continues. Guests in the second half-hour will be folksinger Wireguts Rafferty, who opens tonight at The Baked Potato; Orville Snook, founder of the Gull Watchers Association in Spit Harbour, New Brunswick; and visiting British novelist Violet ffrench-Wyndough, who has just completed ten weeks at the top of the best-sellers list with her latest book *Through a Glass Darkly.*

4:30 *Wreckage,* a radiophonic poem by H. E. Teperman: the text is aleatoric, and consists of syllables improvised by Method students from the Drama Workshop at the Community College for Performing Arts and Constructive Play, in Climax, B.C.; and the incidental score consists of Found Music, mainly metallic, recorded in the Rusty Skidoo junkyard at Dorsal Inlet, Northwest Territories. Producer, Jane Fragment.

Joyce Parchment's bosom came into the office, followed at a distance by the rest of Joyce Parchment. In other respects she was a quite petite woman, fragile almost. This accented her mammary profusion to the verge of absurdity. And Inspector Coggin, who had a keen eye for detail, noted that she was wearing flat shoes: high heels would have launched her, precipitate and helpless, onto the rug. She sat down, carefully; lit a cigarette, cool and businesslike; and said, "Yes, gentlemen. What can I do for you?"

They introduced themselves. Then, patiently but necessarily, they went over the well-worn ground yet again, and learnt nothing new. That done, Sergeant Sump asked one of his usual general questions: "To your knowledge, did Mr. Midden have any enemies in his professional life?"

She snorted harshly. "Yes, hundreds. In fact, I would say the word 'enmity' accurately describes the attitude of just about everyone who had to work with him. But if you mean, did anyone hate him enough to kill him, I simply don't know. And the same holds good for his private life too: he was a pretty hateful person; but I don't know of anyone who'd have gone that far. I wouldn't have thought so. Most people don't act out their fantasies that way. But I guess I was wrong, wasn't I?"

"Yes, I'm afraid you were." Sergeant Sump was ceasing to be surprised at the readiness with which people spoke of their dislike for the dead man. "How about yourself? Did you hate him?"

"Sure. I loathed his guts. But I didn't kill him."

"Why?"

"Because he wasn't worth the trouble, or the risk."

"No, I meant, why did you hate him?"

"Oh, I see." She stubbed her cigarette. "He'd raped me."

This was said in a flat voice, without perturbation, and Sergeant Sump found her calm far more unsettling than agitation would have been, or even hysteria—and far more interesting.

"Well," he said, "if you don't find the subject too painful, I'd like to go into that a little. What happened? When was this?"

"About a year ago. I was still in Personnel at the time. They were looking for a new director for the FM Network, and Henry had to consult with me about the correct way to deal with candidates vis-à-vis the Appointments Board. He said he was tied up during office hours, which seemed very likely true, so he invited me out to dinner. I thought nothing of it, and accepted; after all, he was old enough to be my father." She lit another cigarette. "Well, over dinner we got our business discussed. And he was being rather hammily charming all the time, but I figured that was just reflex: an older man going through the motions, to convince himself he would if he could. Anyhow, it cut no ice with me: not my type. So, after we left the restaurant, he drove me home; and I invited him in for a drink—it seemed only polite, under the circumstances. And I should say here, as far as I was concerned, it was purely a social drink between colleagues: there was no way he could read any kind of come-on into it. At least, that's what *I* thought. But after a couple of belts, he started laying all these heavy passes on me, and I made it perfectly clear I wasn't interested. But the more I tried to turn him off, the worse he got; and when I finally got the message through that I wasn't going to come across, goddammit if he didn't resort to force. And there wasn't much I could do. I was alone in the house, so screaming wouldn't have helped. And fighting back wouldn't have got me anywhere: not against a brute that size—you'd never have guessed his age from the strength he had." She exhaled acridly. "Do you know what I remember noticing at the time? Ridiculous, really. He couldn't even be bothered to take off his shoes."

Sergeant Sump, gently: "Did you consider laying charges?"

"Are you kidding, Sergeant? You should know enough of what goes on in a rape case to know what that suggestion's worth. Half the time it's the woman on trial, not the man. And even if the man *is* convicted, punishing *him* can't cancel out the trauma *she's* been through. And it's not as if there's ever any compensation. No, we didn't consider laying charges. We decided we'd find our own way to get compensation."

"We?"

"Yes. Me and the 'friend' I live with."

Sergeant Sump caught the inverted commas around *friend*. "He must have been pretty upset. Your 'friend,' I mean."

She looked back at him levelly. "Why do you men always assume that if a woman chooses to share her life with someone, it has to be a man? My 'friend' is a very distinguished woman broadcaster, and I may say, yes, she was extremely upset. She came home just as Henry was . . . finishing; caught him in the act."

Sergeant Sump felt rebuked, and rightly, for his lack of tact. But Inspector Coggin rescued him. "You said just now that you and this lady—what's her name, by the way?"

"Amanda Clinch. She's head of Religious Programs."

"Thank you. Yes: you were saying that you and she decided to find your own way to get compensation. You realise, of course, what sort of light is shed on that statement by last night's killing?"

"Certainly I do." She was unruffled. "It means you think we killed him. But I also realise you have to prove it. Which you can't do, because there isn't any proof. Because we didn't do it. And if you just want to go by motive and arrest everyone who had a reason to kill him, you'll have a bigger herd than a cattleman at roundup time."

At the moment Inspector Coggin didn't have an answer to that. Sergeant Sump resumed: "Yes, but just what was it that you did decide to do?"

"Oh, nothing melodramatic like revenge. Just a little *quid pro quo*. After what I'd gone through, it seemed fair enough that he should have to come across too. So Mandy suggested we tell him to give me the FM Network: if he didn't, we'd lay charges. Needless to say, he didn't give us any trouble."

"So I guess you considered the account was settled, then. You didn't push for anything further?"

She stiffened. "What do you mean?"

"Well, everyone's been telling us all day how close to retirement Mr. Midden was. I wondered if maybe you'd told him you'd also like to move up to *his* job when he quit."

"Whatever gave you that idea?" She seemed genuinely surprised.

"Let's just say I'm paid to speculate. So you didn't, eh?"

"No, Sergeant, I didn't. And I wouldn't have got very far if I had. Henry could have recommended me till he was blue in the face, but nothing would have come of it. The choice lies with the president. And not in a million years would President Laval have given that job to me. Not even if *everyone* said I was right for it."

"Any particular reason?"

"Yes. I was married to his stepson—which was a bad mistake, for both of us. And when we found out that men aren't really my cup of tea, Claude divorced me. But I was awarded custody—we had a daughter. And Claude went into a terrible depression and ended up shooting himself. With a hunting rifle. In the Lavals' cottage. His stepfather found the body. He also found a suicide note, which blamed me for everything. He's never forgiven me. So you can put that speculation to rest, about my thinking I might have had a crack at Henry's job."

Neither of them thought it necessary to tell her about Henry Midden's memo, recommending her to the president. It didn't make sense, in connection with what she'd just said. Yet she had sounded plausible enough. Or was she, perhaps, just good at sounding plausible? Certainly a rape victim who could parlay her violation into a promotion was a pretty cool customer. This would bear further thinking about.

Inspector Coggin left these questions in the air, and went back to factual matters. "Perhaps we could pick up last night again where we left off," he said. "After the meeting was over, what did you do?"

"Drove home. And I didn't waste any time either. My daughter had come home yesterday for a couple of weeks (she's in second year at Dalhousie), and I really didn't want to have to work late the first evening she was home. However, there wasn't anything I could do about it. So I just went home as soon as I could. We stayed up late, talking."

"How late?"

"Oh, about half-past two. Then I had to go out again. Catherine came with me."

"Where to?"

"Back here. Mandy was working late, so we'd promised to come down and pick her up. She hadn't seen Catherine since Christmas; they're very fond of each other."

Inspector Coggin did not pursue the implications of that: he felt unequipped to probe child-parent relationships in a lesbian ménage; instead, he stayed with what he did best, an investigation of incident. "So you left the house at half-past two. When did you get here? What did you do while you were here? And how long did you stay? I'd like as much detail as you can remember, please."

"All right. Well, to begin with, we arrived at three o'clock. I know that's when it was, because I checked my watch when we arrived, because three was when we were due here, because that's when Mandy's studio booking ended. Can you imagine, Inspector, an operation this size and we have only one studio with halfway decent tape-mixing facilities? It's booked solid, twenty-four hours round the clock. Mandy had a final mixing session to attend, of a big religious drama, and the only time she could get in there was from one A.M. to three."[1]

Leisurely digression was not a method which Inspector Coggin favoured. "So you arrived at three. First of all, where did you park?"

"In my usual spot, in the executive lot, right outside this window."

"Now I want you to search your memory very carefully. To get onto this lot, you have to go past this building, turn in, and drive around the back and up the other side. Can you recall noticing if there was a car parked on the street, outside the front door?"

"Not then, no. I know there wasn't, because a few minutes

---

[1] Religious broadcasts, at the CBC, had for years a somewhat menial function, to serve as an outlet for the homiletic or liturgical needs of various faiths and denominations, on an equal-time basis. Broadcasts of this sort can be typified by citing one series, "Praise Be!" which was described in the press release as "that old-time religion in its weekly churchathon." The program of the previous Sunday had been listed as "from Bible College in Carbuncle, Alberta, a worship-service of outreach and witness; with inspirational music by the Minstrel Boyles (special solos: Herman Zwonk, electric trumpet), and a scripture-travelogue "With Reverend Tibbs through Darkest Calgary"; also featuring the Repentance Preacher, evangelist Alleluia Verity—her subject "God's Laundry of the Mind." Programs of this sort had survived as sacred cows, unassailably. But their future on the AM Network was assured when that network, in the 1970s, adopted an openly Pop philosophy.

However, during the same period, the Religious Department took on a new importance, on FM, as an outlet for creative programming. These were the years in which serious drama and music were being torpedoed by managerial philistinism. Producers found a way to keep their disciplines alive, despite this trend, by mounting broadcasts of religious plays and oratorios for Amanda Clinch. For instance, the mixing session of the previous night had been of a production by Michael Sherriff of Axel Sorensen's famous existentialist passion play *The Question of Free Will and the Five Wounds.*

later there was. Ordinarily I probably wouldn't have noticed, but this was Bud Benedict's white Mercedes and I'd know it anywhere."

"I see. Thank you." That confirmed Bud Benedict's account. "Now, when you and your daughter arrived and parked, what did you do?"

"Catherine went into the Production Building to fetch Mandy, and I told her I'd wait in the car."

"And did you?"

She sighed and started her third cigarette. "No, I didn't. I was out of cigarettes, and the lights were on in Henry's office, and neither Catherine nor Mandy smokes, so I thought I'd come in and bum a cigarette off Henry if he was in."

"And was he?"

"Yes." She took a drag. "But I couldn't bum a cigarette off him. He was dead."

This was said coldly, almost with indifference. Sergeant Sump was eager to question her about her reactions at the time, and since; but he had to wait his turn, while Inspector Coggin pursued his own line of questioning. The inspector was interested in a lot of detail, but nothing of apparent significance emerged from the answers: the body was seated at the desk, the way Miss Vulpitude had found it later; it was obvious he was dead; no weapon was visible, and there was no sign of the attacker; she had left quickly, and she really couldn't say if she'd turned the lights out or not when she left, it's the sort of thing you're not conscious of; she'd gone out by the rear exit since it was closest to the parking lot, had got back into her car, and had locked the door.

"Needless to say," she concluded, "I was looking around quite carefully while I went to the car. I didn't particularly want to get hit on the head from behind by whoever had done it. That was when I noticed Bud Benedict's car parked out front. It hadn't been there before. And just after I got back into my own car, Bud emerged from the front door and walked down the front path to his car and got in and drove away."

It all fitted together: either this was the truth or else it was a very intricate form of collusion.

"Then, a couple of minutes later, Catherine and Mandy came out of the Production Building over to the car, and we went home."

Sergeant Sump at last could get a word in. "Just like that? You didn't do anything about it, or call for help, or take steps to report it? You just drove home. Didn't you at least tell them about it, and discuss it?"

She looked at him coolly. "No, I didn't. I figured he'd be found in due course anyway, and I wasn't about to spoil my daughter's homecoming with that kind of crap. Oh sure, Mandy and I discussed it after Catherine had gone to bed. She agreed with me." Her mouth hardened, and she added, "That sounds cold-blooded to you, doesn't it? Well, let me tell you, when a man's raped you, you couldn't care less whether he lives or dies. To me, Henry Midden was a piece of shit, and the world's better off without him."

"And your 'friend' agrees with you?"

"Mandy? Yes. I'm quite sure she does."

"To the point, perhaps, of having helped you do it?" Sergeant Sump was not indulging in gratuitous altercation; he simply wanted to break down this woman's defences, sap her self-control. Under stress, people are more revealing, if there is anything to reveal. He succeeded.

"You just try it, Sergeant," she said angrily. "You just try pinning this on Mandy and you won't know whether you're coming or going by the time our lawyer's through with you. There'll be wrongful arrest for starters, and defamation of character, and malicious prosecution; he'll have you busted so fast you won't know what hit you."

Inspector Coggin intervened. "I can assure you, Miss Parchment," he said formally, "we never lay charges unless we have a case that's sure to stand up. However, since this has obviously touched a sensitive nerve, perhaps you'd care to tell us what

157

you know of Miss Clinch's movements last night. Prior to three o'clock."

Her reply was almost a sneer. "Oh, she's covered all right, don't worry; there's no way you'll be able to frame her. She spent the whole evening till one o'clock with a new producer she's hired, name of Mavis Bachelor,[2] going over program materials. Then took her with her to studio 3 to sit in on a nice, sophisticated multitrack mix. They were both there throughout. You can ask the producer, Michael Sherriff."

"Thank you, we will. And if, as you say, she's covered, you won't be needing your lawyer. At least, not for her."

"Meaning I may for myself? Oh come on, Inspector, you don't really think you can make a case against me, do you? We arrive at three o'clock; I get my daughter to go into the Production Building; I notice Henry's in (which I couldn't possibly have known in advance); I sneak in, picking up a hammer en route, which just happens to be lying around conveniently. I pay no attention to the fact that Henry outweighs me by a hundred pounds, and I bash his brains in. I then quickly hide the weapon (have you found it yet, by the way?), and am back in my car inside five minutes. All this, mark you, in a sudden fit of ungovernable rage over a rape that happened twelve months ago. It's laughable."

"It's also physically possible," the inspector replied; "and I've long since given up trying to puzzle out the mysteries of human behaviour. But in answer to your question, no, we haven't found the weapon yet. And I take it, from your attitude, that you'd like us to obtain a warrant if we want to search your car and your home."

She looked at him, for the first time, with misgiving. "Jesus,"

[2] One of five recruits, all female, hired in the Religious Department since the appointment of Amanda Clinch. Natural attrition (deaths, retirements, transfers) had by this time left only one male on the department payroll, a Zen Buddhist from Amsterdam called Wim Vanderknokke, formerly known on the grapevine as the Dutch Treat, but now more commonly referred to as the Finger in the Dykes.

she exclaimed, "you really mean it, don't you? You really mean it."

"Let's say, we intend to cover all the possibilities," Inspector Coggin said. "Frankly, Miss Parchment, it's my guess that you'll turn out to be completely innocent. Guilty people seldom go out of their way to deliberately antagonise the police: your particular brand of discourtesy argues quite strongly against your guilt."

"Oh, there's nothing so special about it," she replied. "It's just that I get pissed off with the world of men. It's always the woman who has to pay. But shit, you can have your search without a warrant if it's going to make you happy. I've nothing to hide."

"Thank you. I think that'll be all, then, for now. Sergeant, perhaps you'd arrange for that to be taken care of. With a warrant."

The interview over, Joyce Parchment left the room—leaning, as usual, slightly forward. Sergeant Sump accompanied her, to detail a man for the search.

Inspector Coggin, meanwhile, picked up the phone and checked in for a progress report. He was still on the phone when Sergeant Sump came back in; and when he hung up, his look was discouraging.

"Just checking in," he said, "and everyone seems to be in the clear. Dammit, Fred, everyone. First off, all the out-of-towners are accounted for: Laval spent the evening at an A.A. meeting, and then was up till all hours counselling a member who's on the verge of a relapse. Hoyle was at a Vancouver dinner party till after the last Toronto plane had left. Same kind of alibi for all the other possibles in other centres. Then there's our bunch here.

"Stukely went on elsewhere with our enforcer friend, after they left the card game, and I shouldn't wonder if he's into something shady, but there are several witnesses that he stuck around where he was; so he's out of it. Furbelow's talked to

Mrs. Casement and she confirms that her husband came home when he said he did; and he couldn't have slipped out again later, because she had insomnia and was wide awake. Gloss has a perfect alibi without knowing it: his stepdaughter confirms that he was in the living room when she came in at two-thirty, as he said. What he doesn't know is that she'd spent the last two and a half hours necking with her boy friend in his car in the driveway, and if Gloss had left the house she couldn't have helped noticing. Benedict's covered, coming and going, by Master Pantywaist; and what he said about turning up here later on jibes exactly with Parchment's sighting of him—just as her movements fit in exactly with his account. And I'll bet my bottom dollar you won't find a blood-stained weapon in her possession; and her 'friend' has obviously got an ironclad alibi too.

"Besides, according to the medical report, death took place between eleven o'clock and two A.M., so it isn't much use placing anyone here at three o'clock, like Benedict or Parchment. So it looks as though we've run out of candidates. Maybe it wasn't a colleague that killed him, after all: just someone who knew him privately, but killed him here to make it look like the act of a colleague. Anyhow, the way I see it, we're back to square one."

"And you remember who was on square one, don't you, Andrew?"

"No. Who do you mean?"

"Miss Vulpitude."

"Oh come on, Fred, you don't really think . . ."

He was interrupted by a knock at the door. Miss Vulpitude came in. "It's five o'clock, Inspector," she said. "If there's anything I can do to be helpful, I'd be glad to stay on. But if not, perhaps I could be on my way."

"Well, I'd appreciate it if you could stay on for a few minutes," Inspector Coggin replied. "We needn't keep you long. But there are a few things you may be able to help us with."

ELEVEN

Tuesday, 5:00–6:00

PROGRAM SCHEDULE #10: 5:00–6:00

5:00 News

5:04 "Yours Truly" continues. Guests in the second hour will
be Jock Reekie of Butt Haven, Vancouver Island, who is
on a coast-to-coast tour as spokesman for CURSE (Cigarette Users' Right to Smoke Everywhere); columnist
Grace Feathers, with an item on how Astral Rhythms
can help your dating; jazz-drummer Skull Bezique, currently rehearsing with the TSO for a performance of
Hit, his new concerto for traps and orchestra; home-
maker Desmond Lavender with a new recipe for Cherry
Mousse; and film critic Spud Grogan talks about the latest trend in movies, Porno-Nostalgia, and the new block-
buster "Cleavage 1948."

5:00 "Première": a series devoted to Canadian compositions
not previously broadcast. This week, two works: "Ab-
straction and Concretion" for nine-note scale, dice cup,
and tone-generator, by Lise Paquette of Mont-Ranvier,
Québec, realised by the composer; and "Élégie Mon-
tagnarde" for soprano voice and bass clarinet, by Todd
Bergseigers of Widow's Peak, B.C., performed by Do-
lores del Caída and Mort Felstein. Producer, Granville
Hobbs.

5:30   "Début": a series devoted to Canadian performers not
previously heard on the air. This week, three artists:
Jerome Sharp of Port Willis, Ontario, will play the Bar-
tók sonata for unaccompanied violin; Christine Kreuz of
Armstrong, Manitoba, will sing three Brahms lieder; and
Pierre Dièse of Lac-la-Bouche, New Brunswick, will play
Chopin waltzes. Producer, Jan Hluchota.

"Miss Vulpitude," Inspector Coggin began, "we've been hearing other people's opinions of Mr. Midden all day. In a way, that's going to be very helpful: if we have a reasonably good portrait of the victim, we stand a much better chance of being able to figure out who might have wanted to kill him. But a composite portrait by other people is never as complete as we'd like it to be. There are always a lot of gaps. So I was wondering if you could give me access to any tapes or documents of Mr. Midden's which might, at least partially, provide a sort of self-portrait we could examine."

"I can certainly try," she replied. "Let me see. I have his complete correspondence for the last twelve months, and the president says you can see anything like that which you might want to. So there's that. And then he had to make speeches every now and again, and I've got the texts of them. But I'm afraid tapes might be a bit difficult. You see, every time I finished transcribing one of his tapes I used to erase it for re-use. So the tape you found this morning is the only one there is. No, wait a minute. There's a whole pile of others: big tapes. I forgot. Two months ago he chaired a conference on the

Radio Future of Music and Drama and Features. The whole thing was taped"—she got up and crossed the room and opened a cupboard—"and we have all the tapes here." She pointed to them and pulled out a bulky, bound typescript. "If you want to listen to any of them, to kind of get the feel of his personality, just take them over to the Production Building and set them up on one of the machines in the listening rooms—we can get someone to show you how, if you like. But, of course, reading's a lot quicker; so if you glance through the transcript, you'll probably get a pretty fair idea of some aspects of the man." She laid it on the corner of the desk beside him.

The telephone lit up. Sergeant Sump answered it, identified himself, and listened. After a moment they saw his face register surprise and puzzlement. Then he said, "Excuse me, sir, I'd like to take this on the other extension." He put the phone on Hold, got up, and left the room, closing the door behind him.

Inspector Coggin was disinclined to pursue any important questioning without Sergeant Sump present. Besides, he was tired, from a long afternoon of concentration. Miss Vulpitude sensed a relaxation in him, a probable openness to small talk. "Pity it isn't the Oval Office," she said.

"The what?"

"The Oval Office: in the White House. You know, Watergate and all that. If it were, everything'd be recorded, and you'd have all the tapes you could possibly want."

"Yes, I suppose so."

"Good Lord," she went on, "if we had something like that and it was left switched on, there might even be a record of who the murderer was—without his knowing. Oh well, wishful thinking, eh?"

"Yes."

"By the way, Inspector, talking of Watergate, did you happen to hear that tape test we did on one of our programs, right around the time when everyone was wondering if Nixon had meddled with his tapes?"

"No, I can't say I did."

"It was very interesting. What we did was take a recording of two people talking in a room—spontaneously: they didn't know they were being taped. Then we edited the tape, cutting hunks out of it as skilfully as we could. Then we sent a splice-free dub of it to two tape experts in the FBI and asked them to try and spot where it had been edited. Then, when they said they were ready, we put them on the air, played the tape, and invited them to spot where the edits were. Well, they failed to spot any single edit we'd made. And not only that, the one place where they did say, quite confidently, there had been an edit, they were wrong: it sounded funny, all right, but actually all it was was a peculiar inflection of the person who was speaking on the original tape."

"Fascinating," the inspector said. "No wonder tapes aren't admissible as evidence—at least, not if there's any chance they could have been tampered with. As a matter of fact, that's something I've often thought I'd like to look into one day, if I could find the time; and so should our Police College. Do you ever run courses on tape-editing? If you do, it'd be very useful if some of our people could sit in on one of them."

"Oh yes, I should think that could be arranged. We have three-day courses fairly regularly. And incidentally, the engineer who's the instructor on them is the same chap who did the edits on the tape I told you about: George Remisnyk. He does the technical part of it, and a couple of senior producers join in to talk about its application to programs: Granville Hobbs, for music; and Michael Sherriff, for the spoken word."

"Great. Maybe I'll have a word with Mr. Remisnyk later, if he's on today—if he's not completely tied up."

"Sure, I'll give him a call." She pressed the button for the spare local, dialled a number, enquired about the possibilities, and said to the inspector, "He says he's not doing anything in his supper hour at six o'clock, and he could come over here and get you if you'd like to have a snack with him in the cafeteria." And so it was arranged.

Sergeant Sump came back in and sat down. "Miss Vulpitude," he said, "I wonder if I could double-check something with you. You told us earlier that that piece of dictation we found on Mr. Midden's dictaphone this morning hadn't been there when you left work yesterday. That right?"

"Yes."

"And when was that, please?"

"Just after five o'clock."

"And you left to go straight home?"

She smiled wryly. "Yes: if you can call it going 'straight' home, battling through the chaos you fellows think of as Traffic Control."

Sergeant Sump refused to be side-tracked. "What then? After you got home?"

"I had supper." Miss Vulpitude was not long in realising the drift of these questions. "If you like, I can give you a detailed breakdown of what I ate, and how long each item took to cook."

Sergeant Sump acknowledged her irony with a fatherly chuckle. "Oh, I don't think that'll be really necessary. But we do have to have everyone fully accounted for, you realise. Even if it's only a formality. Did you stay in the rest of the evening?"

"Yes. At least till the end of the evening. I went out again about half-past ten. To church."

"At half-past ten?"

"Well, actually by the time I got there I was sorry I hadn't left earlier: the place was full and I had to sit in the rear pew."

"Excuse me, Miss Vulpitude, but that does seem an odd time of night for a church service. Especially on a weekday. What was the occasion?"

"Yes. It was an anniversary. You remember last year when All Saints' Anglican burnt down, up Jarvis Street? Well, I'm a member of the congregation. And ever since, St. Patrick's across the road has made it possible for us to worship there— quite an important step, I'd think, for a Roman Catholic parish to do something like that. Anyway, needless to say, we've been extremely grateful, and it's worked out just fine: not just the convenience of it, but a new spirit of understanding on both sides. So last night was the anniversary of the fire, and we had special services to mark a year of important new friendship, with both collections going towards our Rebuilding Fund. Our service was at eleven o'clock—a solemn eucharist, complete with procession. And it was immediately followed by a midnight mass for the Roman Catholics. A lot of people were present right through: Anglicans staying on for the Roman mass, or R.C.'s coming early for ours. It seemed to fit the spirit of the occasion that way somehow. At least, I felt it did. I stayed on. And many, many others did too."

"I suppose there were plenty of people there who knew you. People who could confirm your attendance." Sergeant Sump was embarrassed: it seemed in poor taste to press the point.

"Oh yes," Miss Vulpitude appeared unoffended. "I could give you the names of several of our parishioners who must have seen me there; including a lady sitting in the same pew—I drove her home afterwards. Then there are members of St. Patrick's who could vouch for me, too. For instance, Michael Sherriff: he came right at the beginning, like a lot of them, though he didn't actually sit with us till later on, as he went to Confession first. The R.C. clergy were doing quite a brisk business with that while our service was going on. Incidentally," she added drily, "there's a pretty fair contingent from CBC that attends St. Patrick's: we aren't all a bunch of godless perverts, whatever they say in Parliament. The only odd thing about it is that, so far as I know, none of the members of the Religious Department are churchgoers."

Inspector Coggin, as usual, wanted to know about times. "You say you left home about ten-thirty. When did you get to St. Patrick's? And when did the services end? And how long did it take to drive this other lady home? And when did you finally get back to your place? As nearly as you can figure."

"Five to eleven. One o'clock. Forty minutes. And ten past

two," said Miss Vulpitude, answering the questions in order and not wasting any breath. Inspector Coggin just managed to keep up with her in his notebook. He then obtained from her the name, address, and phone number of the fellow worshipper whom she'd driven home, shut his notebook, and turned to Sergeant Sump. "I think that's about it, isn't it, Sergeant?"

"Yes, I guess so," the sergeant said. "Oh well, just one more thing, Miss Vulpitude. How long have you had your present typewriter? And can you remember roughly when it was last serviced?"

"Three years," she said. "And April the twenty-third. Easy to remember that date because the maintenance man went on at some length about its being Shakespeare's birthday, and Mr. Midden, of course, was quite unaware that it was."

And on that ironic note, she left.

"What was that all about, Fred?" the inspector asked. "The typewriter, I mean."

"Just checking," the sergeant replied. "That was the president on the phone. And I had to take the call on the other extension, so Miss Vulpitude wouldn't hear what I was saying. You'll never guess what he had to tell me. He'd flown back to Ottawa right after he left here; and got to his office a few minutes ago; and there, sitting in his in-tray, delivered this afternoon, was Midden's memo. The one we found on the dictaphone. Which Miss Vulpitude said she hadn't transcribed."

"What!"

"And he'd no idea, of course, that it wasn't sent out, in the ordinary way, before Midden died. He didn't realise the significance of that aspect of it at all. But he phoned me about it because he'd read it, and he figured we ought to know what it contained, in case it would help us with our investigation."

"So what did you tell him?"

"That we had a copy here, so he didn't need to read it to me. But I asked him to describe it to me, physically, and he said it had the normal layout any memo would have: the usual formula at the bottom, with Midden's initials in upper case and Miss Vulpitude's after them in lower case; and it was signed with a rubber-stamp signature—which he says was quite habitual with Midden's memos."

"Anything else?"

"Only this. The date on it, he said, was yesterday. I didn't know quite what to make of that; so after I was through talking to him, I made a couple of enquiries at the CBC mailroom. And apparently there's no way they can do a trace on it after delivery if it went the normal route. If it went off yesterday before five (which we hadn't figured on, but I'll get to that in a moment) it would catch the evening plane to Ottawa: CBC just sends its Ottawa bag up by courier; seems they'd rather not wait three weeks for the post office to get off its butt. Even at that, though, it still wouldn't be on the president's desk until after he'd left to fly down here; so he wouldn't see it till he got back. Okay, that's one possibility.

"The other one is that it didn't go off yesterday before five. If it didn't, there's still nothing extraordinary about its reaching the president by this afternoon: anything that gets into the Otawa bag by nine-thirty goes up on the morning plane; the mailboys here don't do a pickup before nine-thirty, but anyone can put an envelope through the Ottawa slot in the mailroom door and it drops right into the bag without even having to be sorted. And that slot's accessible right through the night, to anyone. Good and handy to here, too: just a few yards from the back door of this building, down at the dark end of the parking lot; on its own with no security post nearby. Nice, eh?"

"Delightful." The inspector sighed. "Getting back to your conversation with the president, was he able to contribute anything helpful?"

"In the way of information, no, not really. But he was quite co-operative, compared with earlier on. So I asked him not to handle the memo any more, in case there are any identifiable fingerprints on it besides his. And I asked him to dig out a couple of other recent memos from Midden, so we can compare if they were typed on the same typewriter. And I've arranged for the Ottawa force to pick them up and run the tests right away."

"Good. H'm, so that's why you went after Miss Vulpitude when you came back in."

"Yes." Sergeant Sump sighed. "She seems pretty well covered later on, around the time of the killing, if her witnesses back her up. But you'll notice she isn't so well covered earlier on: no one to back her up between five and eleven. And not only that; we've also only her word for it that that reel wasn't recorded before five o'clock. For all we know, Midden could have dictated it yesterday morning, and she could have typed it up and sent it off right away."

"That's true."

"The trouble is, though, we don't know what her involvement might be, if any, or why. Look, Andrew, do you think there's any possibility we're wrong in just looking at a murder because that's what we're faced with? Suppose there's actually more than one crime—or, anyway, more than one occurrence."

"What do you mean?" Inspector Coggin asked.

"This. Occurrence number 1: Midden dictates a memo slamming everyone except the Parchment woman, and it's no use to her for reasons she's explained. Occurrence number 2: Midden is murdered. So we have to develop a theory which explains both occurrences. But that doesn't mean they have to be directly connected. Right?"

"Not necessarily. Carry on, Fred. You may be on to something."

"Well, just for the sake of hypothesis, how about this? Midden dictates the memo. Miss Vulpitude transcribes it and gets in touch with the four men it attacks: Stukely, Casement, Gloss, and Benedict. They decide that Midden has to be killed, to save their careers. Stukely volunteers to set this up, which ex-

plains his getting together with our enforcer friend. But he realises it may take a day or two, so they just ask Miss Vulpitude
to hold off sending the memo while they find themselves a
killer. But then Miss Vulpitude has an attack of conscience, or
cowardice, so she sends the memo off anyway, as that's the best
way of stopping the murder taking place—once the memo had
arrived the damage would be done and there'd be no point in
the killing. Okay so far?"

"Yes."

"*Meanwhile*, entirely by coincidence, the Parchment-Clinch
twosome may have been planning for a very long time to have
Midden knocked off, to pay him off for the rape. And when I
say 'a very long time,' I mean ever since the rape happened.
But they were smart enough to let a lot of time go by, so no
one would make a connection between the rape and the killing.
You know as well as I do, the gay world and the criminal world
overlap: it's entirely possible those two women mix in the cir-
cles where they'd know a hit man who'd be willing to take on a
contract. If so, you'll notice both of them had taken the trouble to have a cast-iron alibi for last night, for the hours that
mattered."

He paused, and then summed up. "That's what I mean
about there not having to be a direct connection between Occurrence number 1 and Occurrence number 2. On the one
hand, the four men plan to kill Midden, with the co-operation
of Miss Vulpitude; but she backs out, and the plan is never
fulfilled. And on the other hand, the two women also plan to
kill Midden, for an entirely different reason, and succeed in
doing so. What's confused us all day is that the two elements
happened to meet in timing. What do you think?"

"I think it sounds very good, Fred. It's not the only possibility, but it's certainly a plausible one. Of course, as you say,
it's pure theory as yet. You'll have to do a lot of spadework if
you're going to plug the holes in it. For instance, you'll want a

weapon, preferably in Parchment's possession, or Clinch's; you'll have to trace your hit man; and you'll have to figure out how they set Midden up for the kill. I mean, they had to count on his being in his office at that ungodly hour."

Sergeant Sump smiled. "Oh, I think we can guess the answer to that one, without necessarily ever being able to prove it. All it'd take would be one seductively voiced phone call to Midden, suggesting a midnight assignation, and from what we hear he'd come running so fast you wouldn't see him for smoke."

The inspector nodded. "I guess so. Anyhow, let me know how the boys get on with the weapon search: I'll be here for a while, and I'll leave word where I can be reached when I go. And you might have someone drop in"—he consulted his notebook—"on Miss Farthing in Mississauga, to check if she can confirm Miss Vulpitude's presence in St. Patrick's. Here's the address." He scribbled it out and handed it over. "And one thing I'd like you to do yourself is go over to St. Patrick's and take a look at the place. I'm wondering if there's any way Miss Vulpitude could have sneaked out without being noticed, for a few minutes, and come back across the road and knocked off Midden herself. After all, she did say she was sitting in the rear pew. Admittedly, it's a little hard to imagine how she might have managed it, without Miss Farthing noticing. But you know more about things like Catholic masses than I do, so something may cross your mind which wouldn't occur to me."

"Sure, I'll go over there. I'd be interested to, anyway. But as for slipping out unnoticed, I can suggest how she could manage that without even bothering to go over there and look. Have you ever been to a High Anglican mass?"

"No, I can't say I have."

"Well, I haven't exactly made a habit of it myself. But the couple of times I have been, it seems quite like the way our masses used to be before Vatican II turned everything around. In fact, when all those reforms were first introduced, some of our more die-hard parishioners used to say if you wanted to hear a proper mass these days in Toronto you had to go to an Anglican one.[1] Anyhow, what usually happens when it comes time for everyone to take their communion is that they all file out of their pews and line up in the centre aisle to wait their turn. In a big church, if it's full, that can take a good quarter of an hour. The people up front, who get to the altar rail first, after they've had their communion, move around to the side, left and right, and go back down the church by the side aisles, until they reach their pews, and then file into them from the side aisles. Now, if Miss Farthing was in the line-up in front of Miss Vulpitude, and they were the very last in the line-up, Miss Vulpitude could have slipped out the back door of the church without anyone being any the wiser. And she'd have had ten clear minutes before she needed to be back in the line-up, and the chances are good that not a soul would notice. Certainly, if she did do that and came over here and walked in on Midden (having previously arranged for him to be here), she's one person who could go right up to him without his suspecting he was in any danger."

"And what about motive?"

"Motive? The way that man contrived to get himself hated by everyone, I wouldn't be surprised if he'd driven even Miss Vulpitude to the point of murder."

Inspector Coggin sighed. "You know something, Fred?" he said. "I hope you're wrong."

"Uh-huh?"

---

[1] The rector of All Saints' Anglican, Father Gervase Stubbs-Poynton, when asked why he didn't move his altar out from the east wall of the sanctuary, as many less high-church Anglicans did in conformity with the post-conciliar Romans, a change which permitted the priest to address the congregation, replied, "Because I was always under the impression that I was supposed to be talking to God." He also retained the Office of Tenebrae, when the Romans abolished it. And, during the period of sharing premises at St. Patrick's, he found it hard to eschew a somewhat competitive attitude in the use of incense and vestments.

"I was beginning to rather like that lady."[2]

"Me too. But then, it wouldn't be the first time we've been disappointed in people, would it?"

[2] A similar locution, during a previous case, had once earned for the inspector a reproof, from a high school teacher of English, because he had split an infinitive. "Before you go too far out on that limb," he had replied, "I suggest you reread Fowler." The teacher's response was, "Who?" And the only civil reply Coggin could make to that was, "Well, at least you didn't say 'whom.'"

TWELVE

Tuesday, 6:00–8:00

PROGRAM SCHEDULE #11: 6:00–8:30

6:00 World News

6:30 "Your Land and My Land": a trans-Canada hookup of listeners "live" from everywhere, via on-air phone calls to the studio, with government ministers and spokesmen fielding questions and answering criticism on issues of the day; a program of participatory democracy, in which the People confront the Establishment. Tonight's guests, and the questions on which the public should telephone, are as follows:

1/ Mr. Justice Vincent Flitch, of the Supreme Court of Canada: "When hearing landmark cases which concern Women's Rights, why don't male members of the Supreme Court disqualify themselves?"

2/ Hon. Spudley van Horne, Minister of Justice and recently chairperson of the Federal-Provincial conference on highway law: "When a motorist is convicted of drunk driving, why is there not a mandatory and irreversible loss of licence for life?"

3/ His Worship Zak Erb, Reeve of Stubble, Saskatchewan, and President of the Canadian Association of Mayors and Reeves: "What can we do about dog turds?"

Hostperson: Florence Knapp. Production: Luke Oldham.

FM SERVICE

6:00 World News

6:30 "Serial for Supper": each weekday evening at this time, a well-known actor reads one of his favourite books, in instalments; this evening, episode 27 from *The Life-Expectancy of Loxodonta Africana: an Actuarial Approach to Problems in Zoology*, by Garvin Dibble, selected and read by Chuck Woodleigh.

7:00 "Records in Review": discophile Vaughan Burge and music critic Simone Maudite regularly present and discuss some recent issues: this week's special guest is bass-trombone virtuoso Ingemar Bull; and the recordings they've chosen are *Deux Préludes d'après Lully* by Marcel Dupré, played by Amadée Prévost, organ; *Hodie precamus* ("Humbly we do pray thee, Lord, this day") by Josquin Des Prés, sung by the Schola Cantorum de Prades; *Deep River Raga*, with Khuldip Ray; and *Katmandu, Prague, Melbourne: Three Symphonic Landscapes*, played by the Orchestre d'Ypres, conducted by Carlos Allende-Pratella.

By CONTRAST WITH the orderly series of evenly spaced interviews that had occupied the afternoon, the next two hours were spent in somewhat piecemeal fashion, on various and dispersed activities, with each policeman following a separate path.

Inspector Coggin thought wistfully of the roast lamb his wife was probably now about to serve to their guests, with mint sauce and apologies for his absence; but he knew he couldn't go home yet. So, with George Remisnyk, he went to the cafeteria and had stringy stew with cement dumplings, and chatted idly about tape-editing, while waiting for some reports to come in from hither and yon. They finished up their conversation in one of the editing rooms, where Remisnyk demonstrated a few of the techniques that were his consuming interest in life. And then the inspector thanked him and went back to Midden's office to see what progress had been made.

The search of Joyce Parchment's car and of the house she shared with Amanda Clinch, like the search of Henry Midden's office and its surroundings, had failed to produce a murder weapon. This was no surprise. Killers frequently dispose of their weapon, for fear of being traced through it; and if they have the time and opportunity, they usually do so in a place so improbable and remote that the weapon, if it is found at all, is more likely to be found by accident than by searching. Pending further leads, the men on that job were assigned to other duties.

Meanwhile Sergeant Sump, after a quick visit to the motel snack shop across the road, for a leather sandwich and alleged coffee, had moved on next door, to St. Patrick's Church. This edifice, which had been built some seventy years before, when Jarvis Street had still been a fashionable avenue of gentry residences, was an outstanding monument to the bad taste of the time. Pillars of imitation Ionic design, with no functional purpose, rose inappositely before the imitation Romanesque west door; the nave was imitation Gothic, except for the upper story which was imitation Regency; and the chancel, recently transformed in deference to the vogue for renewal, was imitation Bauhaus.

This medley of architectural plagiarisms was coated on the inside with stucco of a peculiarly unappetizing off-white, like decaying cod, and on the outside with locally quarried stone of vast cost and of a pinkish hue reminiscent of domestic vin rosé at its worst—this gave a strangely choleric expression to the gargoyles, which peeped out mediaevally at intervals along the Attic pediment, each of them the portrait of some Edwardian worthy anxious to leave his mark on the spiritual life as well as the commercial. Their wives and daughters, stoutly arrayed in wings and haloes, graced the stained-glass windows, which had obviously been confected by a candy maker with an enthusiasm for the glummer shades of sacred pigment.

The furniture abounded in tortuous knobs and grooves, which had been thought suitable by the conscientious carpenter who had copied them off the more exuberant marble tombstones (imitation rococo) in the nearby cemetery. In the northeast corner of the nave was a Lady chapel, dominated by a garish statue of the Blessed Virgin in plaster, with painted cheeks, which might more suitably have been installed in Disneyland or in a waxwork museum of horrors at the C.N.E.[1] At the west end of the nave's north wall was a large porch, which had been adapted to contain the confessionals, and which was screened from view by a curtain of a woebegone green baize, thick enough to ensure that the devotions of the faithful were not disturbed by the more rousing sins of the penitent. And above the arch at the entrance to the sanctuary, there was a fresco of the Last Supper, which had been painted by a self-taught artist from Belfast, who referred to it as a "muriel": its ancestry was Pre-Raphaelite, via coloured illustrations in cheap magazines; its execution was so entirely lacking in imagination as to have virtually achieved invisibility.

St. Patrick's was high on the list of Historic Buildings to which the Toronto city fathers paid homage, selecting them by the simple formula of age: anything qualified which had been around long enough, regardless of merit; and this allowed the mayor and alderpersons (as they called themselves) to take the credit for cultural benevolence without having to go to any intellectual trouble over it.

Entering this monstrosity, but long since inured to such as-

[1] The Canadian National Exhibition, held annually in Toronto in late August and early September. Its grandiose title was a misnomer. That it was an *exhibition* is true, if we remember the idiom "to make an exhibition of oneself." But that it was *national* would be disputed by citizens resident elsewhere than southern Ontario. And that it was *Canadian* could hardly be maintained, considering that the management invariably insisted on headlining the grandstand show with American entertainers. During the rest of the year, the stadium on the exhibition grounds was home to a small-time football team which relied heavily on American players, and to the local franchise of an American big-league baseball team. In years gone by, as Sergeant Sump sometimes nostalgically remembered, the Police Games had staged a good international track meet here. However, this had been impossible of late, because the track had been ripped out to expand the baseball facilities. It saddened him, this wanton extirpation of a scarce amateur resource for the sake of a professional syndicate. But his sadness turned to anger when he learned that this barbarism was not to be paid for by those who would profit from it but, with the approval of city council, would be charged to public funds.

saults upon the spirit, Sergeant Sump noted that besides the centre aisle there were indeed also the two side-aisles he had guessed at in his hypothesis. Miss Vulpitude could have sneaked out unnoticed, the way he had suggested. He found one of the priests, a Father Curran; he turned out to be the priest who had heard Michael Sherriff's confession the previous evening, and he was able to supply the names of several other CBC staff members who came regularly to St. Patrick's and who had also attended the midnight mass last night. Sergeant Sump thanked him and left; obtained the phone numbers of these people from the CBC Reception desk; contacted several of them, and was assured by them all that Miss Vulpitude had indeed attended too, as she had said. None of them, however, could say they would have noticed if she had slipped out for some reason—she was seated behind them, and they were not in the habit of constantly peering round at their fellow worshippers.

All this Sergeant Sump duly reported to the inspector. Then, at the latter's suggestion, he called it quits for the day. His mind was not likely to cease working on the case, but at least he could put his feet up and enjoy some decently cooked food.

Inspector Coggin stayed on for a while. Less extroverted than Sergeant Sump, he could not so comfortably adjourn, in one quick move, from work to home—he had to allow himself time to wind down. Sitting alone, reflectively, as he was now, in the dead man's office, he could allow his mind to wander back and forth over the case, almost at random. Often enough these sessions of directionless musing would achieve nothing at all, but every now and then they'd be worth it: some neglected fact or unperceived relationship would drift up to the surface of his attention, and progress would be made.[2] He could only wait. And hope.

---

[2] In a subsequent discussion with Michael Sherriff, with whom he had many a conversation after the case was over, he described this process and listened with interest as Sherriff compared it with the process of making a poem: "Poems," he said, "are a way of telling the truth. And the poet's job is to listen, with the utmost patience and attention, to what the poem

On the corner of the desk beside him, there was still lying the transcript of the conference Midden had chaired. He pulled it towards him and flipped it open. He was in no mood to give it thorough study, but he thought it might be worth a glance. It fell open a few pages in, and his eye fell casually on a paragraph of Midden's which began, "If you've been around long enough, you'll realize there's nothing so very new about that proposal. Davidson Dunton's policy, when he was president, antedates it by twenty years. You remember, what he laid down was that we had to strike a proper balance between the use of canned music and using live musicians. Well, we'd all like to go 'live' all the time if we could afford it—I think there's consensus on that. But we'd pay a steepish price if we did. We wouldn't have any budget left over, ever, to spend on drama or features. And I don't think that would go down too well with some of you. So what I'm suggesting to you is that you have to come to terms with this one unavoidable reality: compromise is a fact of life . . . ."

His thoughts wandered off. There didn't seem to be anything much here to bite into. Bland prose. An unoriginal mind. How could he hope to find a lead here? Leads occurred, for Sergeant Sump, in the murky recesses of human personality, unrevealed on public occasions. And, for him, leads occurred in the algebra of fact: to which no piece of bureaucratic bumf could ever be a guide. Nevertheless, he stuffed the transcript in his briefcase. And began to think of leaving now for home.

The telephone lit up, and he took the call. It was the constable who had been assigned to go out to Mississauga. The news was not good. Miss Farthing had died unexpectedly that morning, at an early hour, evidently of a heart attack; her sister had been with her at the time.

Discouraged, Inspector Coggin told the man to go back

---

is trying to tell him about itself. And that seems to be exactly like what you have to do: you have to submit yourself to your case, and listen to what it's trying to tell you about itself. In both instances, the only question the artist has to ask himself is: 'Is it true?' Nothing else matters."

185

there and ask the sister if she had informed Miss Vulpitude; and if so, when. If not, he should get a complete list of everyone she had informed, and ask them if they had passed the news on to her. It might be important to know if Miss Vulpitude had known Miss Farthing was dead—the one person who might with any likelihood have noticed if she had slipped out of St. Patrick's at some point. In addition, he told the constable to phone Sergeant Sump at home and obtain from him the list of churchgoers who had already confirmed Miss Vulpitude's attendance at the church. It would be necessary to contact all of them again, to ask if any of them had seen Miss Vulpitude leaving at the end of the mass by herself or with Miss Farthing. The chances of a useful answer were poor, but the question had to be asked. He hung up.

He sat back in his chair. There was a loose end bothering him, and he couldn't bring it to the surface of his mind: irritating, like having somebody's name on the tip of your tongue. A knock at the door interrupted him, and the junior constable on duty in the outer office poked his head into the room. "It's the cleaning staff, sir," he said. "They want to know if they can come in and clean up."

"Sorry," he replied, "they'll have to wait. But tell them I won't be long. And when I go, you come in with them and keep an eye on them while they're here, okay?"

"Sure." The door closed.

And suddenly there it was, in his own just uttered words: "they'll have to wait." That was it. Why would Joyce Parchment and Amanda Clinch wait a year to carry out their planned killing? That was the hole in Fred's hypothesis. He'd suggested they might have waited for a year or so after the rape occurred, in order to divert suspicion from themselves. But that would only be so if other people knew the rape had happened; there was no evidence that other people did know—that was something which might have to be looked into. If nobody else knew about the rape, they would have had no reason to wait such a long time. Obviously they would wait until Parchment was confirmed in her new job as FM program director. But after that, they would have no reason to wait.

Unless . . . yes, unless she needed time to establish herself in her new job, as a steppingstone to Midden's job when he retired. Had she been lying when she denied having blackmailed Midden for this further plum? If so, she must also have been lying when she ascribed to the president a long-standing grudge against her. No doubt, the basic facts were true, of her broken marriage and her husband's suicide, but conceivably Laval had not held it against her; he may have understood that the fault could not be wholly hers—this, too, might have to be investigated. And if, in fact, the chances of her receiving the further promotion were good, that would explain why Midden, at her insistence, had written a memo recommending her and destroying the candidacy of others; it was not easy, otherwise, to explain why Midden would have done so.

But if all this were so, why would she have killed Midden and not just waited till his retirement? Was she so ambitious that she had to strike while the iron was hot, in case any spanner might later be thrown in the works?

He felt at sea. To answer that kind of question required the sort of intuitive grasp of character that Fred excelled at; not his department. But clearly Fred's hypothesis was going to need a lot of bolstering if it was to be made to stand up.

Evidently, Fred thought so too. For he had not been engaging in idle speculation when he began wondering about the possible guilty involvement of Miss Vulpitude. All leads had to be followed. And in respect of her, there were two possibilities: on the one hand she might have been working entirely on her own, for her own reasons, and everybody else was totally innocent; but on the other hand she might have been working with one or more of the four men, somewhat in the way Fred had guessed at, but not to the extent of being a conscious accessory to murder.

187

This second possibility would bear thinking about. Suppose Miss Vulpitude had transcribed the memo. Shocked by its contents, she had told one or more of its victims what was in it, not knowing what they might consider doing about it, but at least giving them a chance to salvage their careers, if they could, before her monstrous boss succeeded in sinking them all. She had no great opinion of any of them, but she may well have thought Midden had gone too far. Then suppose, too, that these four men (or perhaps not all of them) had stampeded into a murder plot, and that Miss Vulpitude had come to know of this, perhaps accidentally. She would then have sent off the memo, as Fred had suggested, in order to forestall the plot. But she may have been too late. Stukely's enforcer may have found a hit man available to do the job that very night, which would explain why Stukely was tied up with the enforcer later on, to organise the pay-off.

If that were the case, the police might well finish up empty-handed. Unless they could force some of the parties to the plot to break down under questioning. Certainly, looking for a hit man, with no leads to go on, was likely to baffle their efforts.

He felt at a dead end: a day's work, but little to show for it. Time to go home. There comes a point where fatigue and repetition make it pointless to go on. Better to sleep on it. Surprising how some things work themselves out in the subconscious while the intellect is at rest. He got up and fastened the straps on his briefcase.

The telephone lit up. All day Miss Vulpitude had shown a charming talent for showing up on cue: introducing new witnesses just when they were needed, or even appearing in person just when she herself was being thought of; she did not fail him now. He picked up the receiver.

"Coggin here."

"Oh, Inspector, it's Betsy Vulpitude."

"Yes, Miss Vulpitude?"

"Something just occurred to me which I felt you ought to

know. It's probably of no importance at all, but this morning, after you'd played me some of that tape on Mr. Midden's dictaphone, there was something bothering me about it, and I couldn't spot what it was. Well, it's just come to me."

"Yes?"

"As I say, it can't be of any importance. But you and Sergeant Sump may have noticed I didn't seem fully satisfied. Mind you, I'm fully satisfied it was Mr. Midden's voice. There's no doubt about that. I'd know it anywhere."

"But you say something about it bothered you?"

"Yes." She at last came to the point. "Thinking back to it, I've just realised there weren't any mistakes in the grammar. Most of the time when I was transcribing his dictation, I had to fix his grammar for him: it was terrible. Still, I guess everyone has to get lucky once in a while, and this time *he* did."

"But what about the conference transcript, Miss Vulpitude? I've read a little of that, and his English seems perfectly respectable there."

She chuckled. "You try listening to the tape, Inspector: that's a different story. No, it was all cleaned up for publication, too. Just like Hansard. I don't know if you've ever been to a debate in the Legislature and then read the Hansard version afterwards. But I'm afraid most of our esteemed legislators talk like semiliterates, and one of the chief functions of Hansard is to clean up their act."

"That so?"[3]

"Yes." Miss Vulpitude had hoped for a more spirited response, and she was disappointed. "Well, I mustn't keep you. But I thought I ought to let you know, so you'd know it was nothing to bother about. You might have been wondering if perhaps it was something important."

---

[3] Inspector Coggin, in fact, knew that this was so, but he was too tired to engage in any discussion of it. He also knew that the same was true of the House of Commons and the Federal Hansard. And he thoroughly disapproved. To him, it was part of a spreading but deplorable wish to live in a cosmetic universe, instead of in the real world.

"Thanks, Miss Vulpitude. I appreciate it. Well, I guess I'll see you in the morning. Good-bye for now."

"Good night, Inspector."

He wished he knew if she had known she was citing a dead woman as a witness when she had said she had shared a pew with Miss Farthing last night and then had driven her home.

THIRTEEN

Tuesday, 8:00–midnight

PROGRAM SCHEDULE ₩12: 8:00–*midnight*

8:00   News

8:04   "Too Late Thy Morrow": another episode in the con-
tinuing story of Rhoda Corset, her triumphs and tribu-
lations as hospital nurse by day and, after hours, as vul-
nerable woman: starring Dulciana Snivel. Produced by
Horace Gurley.

8:30   "Rock, Folk & Schlock": three cases of pop.
        1/ For trippers, a tour with One Way Acid, thirteen
takes, recorded by the group on their recent country-
wide freakout to every province and territory: from
Bald Top, Baffin Island; Stenson's Landing, Yukon;
Stride, B.C.; Scalp Hills, Alberta; Blood Valley, Sas-
katchewan; Fort Dick, Manitoba; Bunion Township,
Ontario; Cap Nez, Quebec; Spine River, News Bruns-
wick; Gut Cove, Nova Scotia; Montgomery, Prince Ed-
ward Island; Cape Spleen, Labrador; and Placenta Bay,
Newfoundland.
Producer: Al Grotty.
        2/ Highlights from the Spring Folkathon in Lobe-
ville, Manitoba: featuring Hazen ("Cool Arse")
Kruger, Pops Devine, Joyce and Wilma, Hubert and
Edwin, Solitary Tom Cumming, and The Hobbits.
Producer: Jonelle Mallow.
        3/"The Emerald While": from the bandstand of the

Ould Sod Ballroom in glamorous downtown Squamous, B.C., the sophisticated strains of Roger O'Toole and his Irish Swingers, with vocal stylings by Rosie McBride.
Producer: Matthew Glove.

10:00   "The World Today," a wrap-up of the international and national news.

10:20   "Big-Time Sports," with Clutch Ventrum: baseball scores, this year's Triple Crown, and a look ahead at the NFL; time permitting, Canadiana too.

10:30   "Listeners' Choice": ninety minutes of requests, with host Stu Bland; light classics and old favourites, selected by fans who write and tell us what they want to hear. Enclose a stamped envelope so Stu can let you know when your Choice will be aired.

12:00   News.

FM SERVICE

8:00   "The Unmasked Ego," a feature on the use of psycho-drama in the treatment of shyness-syndrome: recorded at the Institute for Normative Behaviour in Skull Point, Ontario, under the direction of Professor Anders Älterung, D. Pharm.; the participants are anonymous.
Production: Guido Martello

9:00   "Community Orchestras," a regular series of concerts from our smaller centres: this week, the Sebastian Ensemble of Scheissenbach, Manitoba, conducted by Art Wagstaffe. The program is especially designed for listeners with quadriphonic decoders, and consists of the

194

Brandenburg Concertos, Nos. 1–4, played simultaneously.
Production: Zelda Klangstreit.

10:00 "The World Today," a wrap-up of the international and national news.

10:20 "The Amateur Ideal," a program for followers of the non-pro sports:

1/ Real Tennis: Foster McVeigh-Tarkington ascribes Canada's poor showing in the World Championships to lack of proper facilities in our major cities.

2/ Track and Field: Russ Withers describes Canada's triumph in the recent dual meet with Luxembourg: our team came home with all the silver medals; next year, Ecuador.

3/ Pelota: the Basque national team swept all its games in last month's tour of Canada: Luiz Queixa blames the Federal Government's failure to finance a proper coaching system.

10:30 "Olla-Podrida," a roundup of news and opinions on the arts in Canada:

1/ Cinema: "The *nouvelle vague* arrives in rural Québec": Antoinette Morue reports from Lac de Loupe in the Gaspé.

2/ Books: Elliott Sturgeon reviews this year's spring list from the Hatchery Press in Duct, B.C.

3/ Broadcasting: "The cult of mediocrity, an independent editorial on trends in AM radio," by Simon Carp.

4/ Music: "The renaissance lute as a factor in prairie chamber music," an outside appraisal by Julius Brill.

5/ Theatre: *Cock-Up* by Rhoda Pike: Wilson Whiting comments on a succès de scandale in Pulse Creek, B.C.
Production: Dwight Fischer.

11:15 "A Cappella," a series of half-hour programs by Canada's unaccompanied choirs. This week, from Sac, New Brunswick, the Rossignol Singers, conducted by Imbert Nightingale: *The Greedy Hawk,* by William Byrd; *Homage to the Soviet Air Force,* by Vladimir Vogel; and *Moultrie,* by Alden Sparrow (CBC commission).
Producer: Raymond Flock.

11:45 "A Thought Before Bed." Each week night at this hour we present thoughts for our time by prominent thinkers: this week's series, "The Eternal Now" by Archbishop Rumpus (retired), speaking from his home in Scarcross in the Yukon; part two, "Ecumenism, Solution or Dilution?"
Producer: Prudence Murch.

12:00 Sign-off.

THINKING OF THE late Miss Farthing and her churchgoing, the inspector made his way across the road to St. Patrick's, before going home, to have a glance at it himself. The church was still open, and the warm evening light crept in sentimentally through the tepid stained-glass windows. He looked around and shuddered. One of the insoluble mysteries of life, to him, was this epidemic paradox: that the devout, who believed in love and reverence and glory, should express their belief through rubbish; it was a denial of the spirit. In this he lacked the charity and understanding of Sergeant Sump: he himself, reserved and ill at ease with most people, could not see the sincerity and good will behind the tastelessness; the sergeant, by contrast, had never thought it likely that decent men or women would be barred from heaven because they preferred "Bless this house" to the St. Matthew Passion. There were no worshippers. A sacristan appeared with keys. It was time to go.

Fred Sump went to bed early. And Andrew Coggin wished he could. But he'd arrived home before the dinner guests had left, and he felt obliged to put in a little time with them. So he took a chicken leg and a glass of wine into the living room and sedated his brain with small talk. They left around quarter to ten, and he headed upstairs to take a shower: his work, white-collar though it was, frequently left him feeling soiled. Towelled dry and relaxed, he climbed into bed; noticed as he did so the crossword puzzle on the bedside table where his wife had put it for him, with its one unsolved clue; solved it without difficulty, as he would have done that morning if he had not been interrupted; and turned out the light.

Mrs. Coggin was a few minutes later coming up to bed, as she had waited for him to finish showering before starting the dishwasher. By the time she got up there he was already fast asleep.

He woke up with a start: fully awake: his question answered. So that was how it was done!

Carefully, so as not to waken his wife, he slid out of bed, added a sweater and socks to his pyjamas, and tiptoed downstairs. The kitchen clock said ten thirty-five. He had had, perhaps, half an hour's sleep. But he felt fully alert and hungry for action.

His briefcase was in the front hall. He took it into the living room, pulled out the conference transcript, and settled into some attentive reading.

Fifteen minutes later he knew that his hunch was confirmed —provisionally. Leaving a note for his wife, he dressed quickly, repacked the briefcase, and drove downtown. It was about ten past eleven when he pulled into the CBC parking lot. The Administration Building was like a morgue—not inappropriately, he thought—except for the constable on duty in Midden's office. He collected the conference tapes from the cupboard where Miss Vulpitude had pointed them out, and headed over to the Production Building.

Here there were a few more signs of life. In the basement a night manager presided over CRAP,[1] the $100,000 machine

[1] This acronym, invented by the engineering staff, stood for "Casement's Ridiculous Automation Project."

198

which was supposed to transmit all the prerecorded programs: it constantly broke down and needed three engineers in attendance as support.[2] On the main floor a receptionist was still on duty; visitors were few at this late hour, but it was also her duty to answer listeners who phoned in to praise or condemn programs or to seek information about them. On the upper floors there was slightly more activity: the cleaning staff were sweeping, dusting, and toting garbage; and an occasional producer was still working late on a program.

Inspector Coggin had the commissionaire take him to the editing room he'd visited with George Remisnyk after supper. The room lacked an air vent and was unbearably stuffy, so he left the door open. Then carefully, and with a novice's awkwardness, he set up the first of the conference tapes on the deck, put on the earphones, and switched on the machine.

It caused him enormous misgiving to attempt, as an amateur, a job that belonged to an expert. But it had to be tried: he had to test his theory.

Fortunately, George Remisnyk had been both lucid and precise. The inspector made a few trial edits in the tape, in contexts which didn't matter; and to his surprise, once he got into the swing of it, he found the work quite easy to do. After a while, his results began to be smooth, accurate, and indetectible. Then, inhaling a deep and nervous breath, he took the plunge.

He ran the tape fast forward until he'd found the paragraph which he'd idly read earlier, in Midden's office, and which he'd more recently reread, with great thoroughness, in his own living room. Miss Vulpitude was right about the grammar: Henry Midden, in that regard, was no different from the current crop of high school graduates (or, as he would probably have put it, "no different than"); but she had done a scrupulous job of cleaning up his text without changing the sense of what he was

[2] Before it was bought, the use of human beings to transmit the prerecorded programs had required the attendance of three engineers. It was thus evident to all, except to CBC Management, that a somewhat less efficient result had been achieved at a cost to the taxpayer of $100,000.

trying to say. This was, however, for present purposes, a trivial matter: the text, in all important respects, was unaltered. From it, carefully, he extrapolated two words: "antedates" and "canned"; from them, trimming and splicing, he made a new word, "candidates." Then, using the same technique, he took three words, "ever" and "Davidson" and "balance," and from them he constructed "evidence." Going on, he constructed "suspicious" from "consensus" and "steepish" and "musicians." He sat back. It had worked.

When you are listening to tapes on earphones, you become much more absorbed in what you are hearing than if you listen to them on a loudspeaker. This is true of all earphones. But it is especially true of the large, heavy kind of earphone, which completely encases the ear: with a pair of these, the listener is completely shut off from the world; a telephone can ring beside him, and he won't hear it. This was the kind of earphone Inspector Coggin was using.

That was why he did not hear the footsteps coming up behind him.

FOURTEEN

Wednesday, 12:04–1:00A.M.

PROGRAM SCHEDULE #13: 12:04–1:00 A.M.

12:04   "The Midnight People": Buzz Rivitt presents tape-interviews with young and old who have something to say. Tonight his theme is Our Changing Lifestyle. And his recorded conversations represent several points of view. An anonymous teen-ager supports marijuana as less damaging than alcohol. A retired etiquette consultant remembers when ladies wore white gloves everywhere. And a fundamentalist clergyman, who disapproves of sex counsellors, defends the recently published pamphlet *What Kind of Sex Does Oral Roberts Suggest?*

1:00   News, weather, and sign-off.

WHEN THE HAND fell on his shoulder, he was profoundly startled. He spun around and whipped off his earphones.

"That sounds interesting," Michael Sherriff observed.

The inspector breathed easier. "How did you know what I was listening to?" he asked.

The producer leaned over and flipped a switch. "You left the speaker on. So the sound was coming through it as well as the earphones. And you left the door open too. I was coming up to my office, and I couldn't help hearing."

"Oh." Coggin was chagrined; he'd done the difficult part, but overlooked something simple. "Well, I don't know how long you've been standing there listening, but so far I've only come up with three words. Still, even with that little to go on, I'd say there's probably a case to make."

"Sure. But how did you get on the track of it?"

"Bernard Shaw's fish," the inspector replied, laconically; and then, answering the incomprehension on Sherriff's face, added, "I'll come on to that later. But first of all, you'll probably be interested to know how thoroughly we were misled to begin with. All day long we've gone on the assumption that the memo we

204

found in Henry Midden's dictaphone . . . you know what I'm talking about, of course?"

"Yes."

"Good. So we assumed that that memo had to be genuine because it was Midden's voice—there didn't seem to be any doubt about that. Then, once we'd assumed it was genuine, a lot else followed: most of the people named in it, for one reason or another, were suspects; and it wasn't impossible that one or more of them might have contrived his death. Certainly we could demonstrate motive: though, the way it looked, we'd find it a lot harder to prove opportunity, or means. Still, for one day's work, so far so good. At least, one might have thought so. But I was bothered. There was something wrong. But I couldn't put my finger on it. That's where Bernard Shaw's fish came in."

"His fish?"

"Yes. You know how strongly he felt about the chaotic way English is spelt. Well, somewhere in his writings he shows how ridiculous it is by proving that *g-h-o-t-i* spells *fish*."

"What?"

"That's right. Phonetically. The *g-h* as in *enough,* the *o* as in *women,* and the *t-i* as in *education.* It was one of our standing jokes when I was in Military Intelligence during the war. Our cryptographers were always having to try and break codes, and any time we were faced with a tough one, we used to call it 'a real Shaw's fish.' As a matter of fact, I invented a code once, which was based on phonetics, and it's my belief that any enemy cryptographer would have had a hard time cracking it, English spelling being what it is. However, as usual, the brass didn't want to innovate."

Sherriff smiled: "You sound like me griping about our Management—so called. But getting back . . ."

"All right: getting back to the point: ever since the war and my code work, I've found it quite easy to solve the sort of cryptic crossword clue that relies on those techniques—transposing letters or syllables, or patching together bits and pieces of various words, or letting the sound of one word or syllable suggest another word or syllable with the same sound but a different meaning. And yesterday's crossword had a clue like that in it, but I didn't get around to solving it until a couple of hours ago. Then, when I did, it must have triggered something in my subconscious, because I woke up half an hour later with a nice shiny new hypothesis all worked out, and everything fell into place."

"And what did your hypothesis posit?"

"This." The inspector was rather pleased with himself, but he tried to keep the complacency out of his voice. "Suppose, I said to myself, somebody had access to a large amount of Henry Midden's voice on tape—such as, for instance, these conference tapes. If he wanted to, he could go over what Midden said on the tapes, and pick out a word here and a phrase there, until he had constructed a whole statement that Midden never made. The only difficult part would be constructing some words which he wanted Midden to 'say' but which he hadn't actually said; however, I've shown that that can be done, by splicing together unconnected syllables—as you know: you caught me at it.

"In other words," he went on, "this somebody could *create* that memo with Midden's own voice, dub it onto a dictaphone tape, and leave it in Midden's dictaphone the night of his death. And everyone would assume that Midden had dictated it."

"As *you* did," Sherriff pointed out.

"Indeed," the inspector admitted. "But it *had* bothered me. At least, once I figured out how it could be done, I realised that was what had been bothering me."

"What bothered you about it?"

"The style."

"Oh." Sherriff looked immediately and suddenly crestfallen.

"Yes, the style didn't fit. I'd never met Midden, but we heard a great deal about him in the course of the day. And from what we heard, I could believe he was bloody-minded enough to write a memo like that; and I could believe in the strange mixture of coarseness and intelligence it contained; but what I couldn't believe, in the light of what everyone told us, was that he could write a memo which showed a real writer's assurance in the handling of English. It simply didn't fit."

"But even supposing all that's so," Sherriff said, "where does that lead you anyway?"

"It leads me into some more supposing," Inspector Coggin replied. "Suppose somebody wanted to kill Midden, one of the best ways to divert suspicion would be to cast suspicion on other people. And a planted memo like that would stir up a whole hornet's nest of suspicions. Right?"

"I guess so."

"And that's a perfectly good motive for our 'someone' to plant the memo. So in order to find out who that someone might be, I had to ask myself two important questions. Who would have had access to a copy of the conference tapes? And who had the necessary technical and creative skills? The answer to the first question was multitudinous: presumably scores of people connected with the conference could have had access to the tapes. But the second question narrowed it down a lot: maybe the CBC had dozens of brilliant producers who could have faked the memo, but you're the only one I happen to have met; and I gather you're the resident expert on the spoken word when they hold tape-editing workshops."

"Interesting, Inspector. But hardly conclusive."

"In itself, no. But I'd hazard a guess that you put so much confidence in the way your fake memo would send us haring off in the wrong direction, that you forgot to cover your own trail properly. For instance, I shouldn't be a bit surprised if a search warrant turned up the edited remains of a copy of the conference tapes either in your office or in your home."

"What if it did? They could perfectly well have been planted there, to frame me."

"Nice try, Mr. Sherriff. But it won't stand up. You see, the trouble is you've already admitted you know about the memo."

"How do you figure that?"

"Quite simply. Ten minutes ago, when we began talking about it, I made a passing allusion to the memo in the dictaphone, and then interrupted myself to ask you casually if you knew what I was referring to, and you said yes you did. I'm afraid that was a fatal piece of carelessness on your part. In addition to that, I shan't be surprised if we find that the typewritten copy of the memo, which the president received, was typed on your typewriter or on one you had ready access to: it probably wouldn't have been easy for you to get at Miss Vulpitude's typewriter just when you needed to, for everything to time out right. Incidentally, I'm sure Sergeant Sump will be relieved if we discover it wasn't typed by Miss Vulpitude. He wasn't any happier than I was to think of her as a suspect."

"Miss Vulpitude!?"

"Yes: Miss Vulpitude. She came under suspicion hours before you did."

"But that's preposterous."

"I agree with you. But murder often is." The inspector paused a moment, and then went on. "However, all I've got so far is a set of postulates. They don't complete the case. They point to you, strongly, though admittedly only circumstantially. But we still have to fill in means and opportunity. As to means, with any luck we'll find the weapon in due course—you may even, in due course, care to tell us what it was and where it is. Opportunity, though: that gave me a lot of trouble, until I turned my thinking upside down."

"How do you mean?"

"Well, you see, it boils down to the need for us to prove opportunity during the two hours or so when the services were being held last night at St. Patrick's. We knew you were there. Miss Vulpitude referred us to you to corroborate her presence there. And that's one of the things that made it a bit difficult to treat her as a likely suspect: figuring out how she might have sneaked out without being noticed, and then presumably sneaked back in. It was workable, but complex and improbable.

And all the time we were figuring that out, it never occurred to me, until a little while ago, to look at that situation the other way up: to ask myself if *you* could have sneaked out and back in again later without *her* noticing. But once I did begin to ask myself that question, it was immediately obvious that you could have done it much more easily than she could. As Sergeant Sump pointed out, it takes a good fifteen minutes for a communicant at the back of the line-up to reach the altar rail. Once Miss Vulpitude was in the line-up, you could easily have slipped out from the rear pew, come across the road, killed Midden and planted the dictaphone tape, dumped the weapon, and been back in your pew before Miss Vulpitude returned from the altar rail."

"Ingenious, Inspector. But not very likely. There'd be far too great a risk that I'd be spotted by someone else, on my way out or in. Anyway, I'm sorry to tell you I can prove you're wrong. I have an impeccable witness, a fellow Catholic, who sat beside me in the pew throughout the time when the Anglicans were taking their communion, and he'll swear I never budged."

"I daresay," said Sergeant Sump from the doorway, having approached unheard on rubber-soled shoes. "But that wasn't how you worked it."

"Hello, Fred," the inspector said. "What brought you here?"

"Well, I got to thinking," he replied. "And I figured out how Mr. Sherriff could manage it, and I couldn't figure out how anyone else could. So I thought I might come down on the off chance he'd be here and we could have a little chat."

Sherriff gestured him into the room. "Join the party. But I fail to see how you can manage to have me in two places at once. I was in the rear pew in St. Patrick's, not budging out of it. So how can you simultaneously have me across the road murdering Henry Midden?"

"I can't. Not simultaneously. But I can a little earlier. At the beginning of the service."

The inspector leaned forward. "How?"

"Like this." Sergeant Sump turned towards Sherriff. "Miss

209

Vulpitude says you arrived at the beginning of the service, but didn't come and sit with her then because you had to go to confession."

"As I can prove. The priest will bear me out."

"He already has. But when I go back to him, he'll no doubt tell me you made a very short confession."

"So what?"

"So this. You disappear from view behind the big green curtain that leads into the porch where the confessionals are. Fifteen minutes later you emerge from behind the curtain and everyone assumes you've made a longish confession. Nobody realises you made a very quick confession and then sneaked out of the north door (yes, I looked: it looked like a porch, and that's exactly what it was); after which you hurried across the road, dispatched Midden, hid the weapon, returned, and came back in through the same door—and into the nave from behind the curtain. And joined Miss Vulpitude. And stayed put. With witnesses."

"You think you can prove this?"

"Very likely. I shall ask Miss Vulpitude whenabouts in the service you joined her; and she's a nice, precise lady. And I shall ask the priest how quickly you made your confession. And if there's ten minutes to spare in there, it'll be up to you to explain what you did with it."

There was a long silence.

"Mr. Sherriff," Inspector Coggin asked, "do you have an explanation?"

"No." He sighed. "I suppose I ought to congratulate you both." He turned to Sergeant Sump. "I don't know how long you were standing there before you spoke up. Did you hear the inspector here explaining about the tape in the dictaphone?"

"No, I didn't," Sergeant Sump admitted.

Inspector Coggin explained.

The sergeant smiled and nodded. And turned back to Sherriff. "What about the weapon?" he asked.

"It's in Studio 5. I brained him with a turntable weight

which I'd put in my briefcase, wiped the blood off with a piece of cloth which I subsequently burnt; and put the weight back in the studio this morning."

"I take it we can have your briefcase then, for analysis?"

Wearily: "I guess so."

The inspector, though, was not yet satisfied. "Mr. Sherriff," he said, "we've figured out how you worked the tape business. And I presume you prepared the tape in advance, and then waited till last night because the St. Patrick's services afforded a clever opportunity. And presumably you called Midden and found a pretext for meeting with him after the evening meeting, so as to be sure he'd be there." Sherriff nodded. "But there's still something missing," the inspector went on, "something important. Motive. Frankly, you haven't impressed me as the kind of man who'd kill out of hatred. Why did you do it?"

"You're right. I disliked him, but he wasn't worth the trouble of hating. And it wasn't fear or revenge or ambition either. But you'll get the answer if you ask yourself the question 'Who stood to gain?' That's a pretty standard question in your line of work, isn't it?"

"Yes," Coggin replied. "But it's usually asked in order to find the culprit. Which we've done. I don't see how . . ."

"Ask it anyway," Sherriff interrupted. "Midden is dead, and a new general manager will have to be appointed. My fake memo has effectively destroyed the chances of the four Toronto men who would have been considered for the job. Even if it was fake, there's enough genuine dynamite in it for it to be effective.[1] And as for the recommendation of Joyce

---

[1] This prediction proved to be fully accurate. Stukely was investigated for corruption, more thoroughly than before, and went to jail, before the Midden murder case was tried. The other three men resigned, after some delicate bargaining: in return for their resignations, Sherriff agreed to plead guilty; which meant that the memo was never made public as evidence. Joyce Parchment was under no pressure from anyone to resign: but did so anyway, not long afterwards, to pursue a freelance career as the foundress and editress (terms she would have rejected) of an unsuccessful magazine called *Dildo*; when last heard from, she was running a feminist bar in Clitterhouse, Alberta, called "The Liquor Trade."

Parchment which it contains, that's meaningless: because, as
you may or may not know, the president detests her and he
wouldn't dream of appointing her. That means all of the obvious candidates are out of the running. And if you go beyond
that list, there's really only one person left in the whole country with the necessary stature and experience. The president
will have no choice. He will *have* to appoint Bill Hoyle, of
Vancouver. So there's your answer. There's who stood to gain."

"You mean, you did this in conspiracy with Bill Hoyle?" Sergeant Sump had immediate and horrified visions of long, fret-
ful conversations with his western counterparts, and tiresome
journeys to and from the coast on a diet of Air Canada's toy
lunches.

"Good God, no!" Sherriff exclaimed. "I simply laid it on so
he'd be sure of getting the job."

"But without his knowledge?"

"Without his knowledge."

Inspector Coggin: "Why?"

"Briefly, Inspector, because he's the only good man we've got
—for that line of work. Not just better than the others. A
different breed. Let me explain."

He lit a cigarette, and continued. "Over the years, as I mentioned to you at lunchtime, we've been plagued by a steadily
deteriorating calibre of management. Radio has gone downhill,
not because of the rise of television, but because the people in
charge have increasingly lacked vision, intelligence, courage, or
standards of taste. At the program level, there didn't seem to
be anything we could do, except carry on as best we could in
spite of them. Each time there was a new administration it
would be a worse one. But each time, necessarily, we'd grit our
teeth and dig in: to give up and resign would somehow be a be-
trayal of what we stood for. However, you can only let things
go so far. There comes a time when you either have to say no
and reverse the trend, or else get out."

He paused to inhale. "I've come to believe that that time is
now. For two reasons. First, the rot has started to seep down

from above and infect the program level: we're now starting to be infiltrated, in the production staff, by thirty-year-old fascists who deride excellence and care only for ratings. Second, the availability of Bill Hoyle represents a real hope that the trend can be reversed: he believes radio's job is to astonish, amuse, enlighten, unify, and if necessary irritate, but not to pacify or sedate. And above all he believes that Canadians, of all backgrounds and tastes, deserve nothing less than the best. You'll hear those same sentiments from all our faceless technocrats, too: they're well schooled in how to parrot the motherhood phrases. But in Bill's case it's a philosophy that would be put to work, not just window dressing."

"Am I to take it, then," Inspector Coggin asked, "that you have committed a murder and ruined the careers of several people simply in order to further the good, as you see it, of radio? I'm not sure whether to call that misplaced idealism or unprecedented arrogance."

"Ordinarily," Sherriff replied with a wry smile, "I doubt if you'd have to call it either. I daresay, in the ordinary course of events, I'd have let this occasion go by too, and watched the CBC degenerate to a point of no return, and become a sour old man complaining about the decay of civilization. Really. Mind you, I do believe that this truly is a turning point in the history of radio. But the chances are, other things being equal, I wouldn't have done anything about it."

"What changed your mind?"

"Illness. I happen to be suffering from a terminal form of cancer. If it weren't for that, I'd probably have hoped to go on producing worthwhile programs, somehow, till the end of my working life, however rotten our management might get. Well, the fates decided otherwise. So I figured, what the hell, if I get caught, a prison hospital's just as comfortable to die in as any other hospital, what's the difference? Then it became an interesting moral question: whether to die with a murder on my conscience or to die knowing I could have done something permanently curative for radio but was too chicken. Well, you

213

know the choice I made. It's my final contribution to a medium I've given my life to."

Inspector Coggin frowned. "In a way," he said, "I respect what you've tried to do. But I think you were profoundly wrong. Nobody has the right to act as you did."

"Possibly so," Sherriff replied. "Certainly that's a position you're bound to take as a police officer, sworn to uphold the law. But unofficially, as a human being, you're intelligent enough to go beyond that. For instance, the only way to stop Hitler was by killing; and you joined the armed forces to do so —even if you didn't ever kill anyone in person yourself. Morally, there's no difference."

"Personally, I think there's a great deal of difference," the inspector countered. "But if we start going into that, we'll be here all night. And I think the time has come now to wrap things up. You realise, of course, we shall have to put you under arrest right away."

"Oh yes, that's quite understood," Sherriff said calmly, stubbing his cigarette. "However, I do have one request. Would it be out of the question for you to wait another ten minutes? I'll tell you why. Because of my illness I haven't taken on a whole slew of future productions. In fact, the program I've been working on has been the last one I was committed to. And it's almost finished. I have it here." He gestured with the tape he'd had in his hand all along. "But I didn't think you'd catch up with me quite so soon. There are three edits left to do, and that's it. They'd take me about ten minutes. Do you think you could stretch a point and let me get them done before we go?"

Inspector Coggin looked over at Sergeant Sump, who shrugged. "All right," he said, and handed over the earphones.

They left the room together, to wait for him outside.